By the same author

The Body Beautiful Murder

The Body
Beautiful Murder

Kin Platt

Random House: New York

All rights reserved under International and Pan-American Copyright
Conventions. Published in the United States by Random House, Inc., New
York, and simultaneously in Canada by Random House of Canada Limited,
Toronto.

Library of Congress Cataloging in Publication Data
Platt, Kin.
The body beautiful murder.
I. Title.
PZ4.P7196Ro [PS3566.L29] 813'.5'4 75-42784
ISBN 0-394-49649-3

Manufactured in the United States of America
9 8 7 6 5 4 3 2

First Edition

The Body Beautiful Murder

One

He came into the gym easing himself sideways through the door, and everybody froze. He wasn't any bigger than a house but he was better-looking, self-made, his own architect. He stood over six feet two, weighed about two hundred and fifty pounds, and his loose-fitting polo shirt couldn't hide the bulging muscles that made his body almost a caricature of the human form.

"Felix Witter," a guy whispered. "Mr. World, Mr. America, Mr. Universe, Mr. Narcissus."

The big guy nodded, smiling, to the goggling muscle men staring at his awesome bulk and walked lithely toward the dressing room, carrying his small canvas gym bag. He came out shortly, wearing buff shorts, nothing on top. The incredibly thick muscles-on-muscles from his neck on down had an almost surrealistic symmetry.

He began pulling out the iron. The barbell at his feet said 350 pounds. He eyed himself in the wall-to-wall mirror, swung the weight up and pressed it ten times for openers.

He had to have thicker biceps than Atlas, more muscle definition than Hercules. I figured him bigger than Achilles and I knew he made more money than Samson the Israelite strong man.

The gym crowd watching him was made up of the usual complement of musclemen: working stiffs trying to stay in shape, those who had gone to pot and were trying to make amends, and the iron freaks, the muscle masochists, the weight lifters and dedicated body builders like Felix Witter. Packing about a 60-inch chest and 22-inch arms over a 34 waist, he made every man in the room look puny. His thighs and calves were like gnarled tree trunks and he looked to be the ultimate in muscular development. With it all, he was blond and good-looking, and carried his pumped-up frame with an easy grace that denied he was a pachyderm lifted out of the Stone Age.

He did four sets of bench presses with a 250-pound weight. He did fifteen repetitions of each set and wasn't breathing hard. Each 45-pound plate looks like a manhole cover. Witter picked them up like boxes of candy, carrying them between his fingers.

He did more sets of presses on an inclined bench with 200-pound barbells. Seventeen "reps" and five sets. He did curls with one hand with 85-pound weights, and leg presses of 500. He was breathing harder now, huffing and puffing with red face and popping eyes, lifting from assorted positions, making each move count, each set violent and running about a minute. The veins in his forearms stood out like ropes. He looked like he was killing himself and enjoying every moment of it.

I had finished my workout and headed for the showers. I came out dressed for the street and he was still at it, his thick torso glistening with sweat.

I leaned close to Les Bundy, the genial gym manager, once a West Coast lifting champ, now carrying a slight paunch over the hard muscles in deference to middle age. "How long does he stay at it?"

Les glanced at the clock over the wall rack of steel bars. "Two hours now. This is his morning workout. He'll work two more later in the afternoon."

"How come he's favoring your gym? I've never seen him work out here before."

Les smiled. "Getting ready for the new Mr. Universe contest. We happen to be more convenient from his new shack in Manhattan Beach. I thought the guys would get a charge out of it. See how hard you have to work to be the best in the field."

4

"He's the best?"

"Mr. America twice. Mr. Europe. Mr. Olympia. Mr. Universe three times. He hasn't lost a competition the last three years. Nobody's ever done four Mr. Universe in a row. If he wins, it makes him the best of all time."

I looked across the room at Witter. He was doing neck curls with a heavy weight that reddened his face. "Any chance he won't win? Somebody from out of left field?"

Les smiled again and shook his head. "The only way they'll beat him is if somebody kills him."

I looked around at some of the faces watching the blond body builder. They weren't all that happy watching him make them look bad. But as a rule, you need more motive for a murder, and looking at Witter's superhuman physique, I thought it would take a very brave or reckless man to try killing him.

I had murders in my own field to contend with, enough to get my mind off Witter. Some sinister and cunning villains were making a shambles of the West Coast drug security measures, knocking our agents off with a tireless zeal and efficiency that suggested big profits as well as a sound organization. When you deal with heroin and cocaine operators, you're taking on the world and its geography. They were funneling in their product from everywhere, always one step ahead of us. Whoever the new Mr. Big was, he was far ahead of my imagination, and the nagging day-to-day frustration he gave me was getting me down. I ran in circles trying to stay on the track but couldn't find a single rabbit to pop.

I had found a bar downtown and was nursing a beer along with a headache when I noticed a small placard. It told me the new Mr. Universe contest was being held at a nearby midtown hotel. It gave the date and time, and I thought if I got off my butt and hurried over, I might see somebody in the flesh being the best in his field. Watching a winner can hype you up sometimes, so I downed the beer and headed my heap for the Hotel Marrot and the convention of musclemen it was hosting.

The Marrot had been elegant and attractive in its time, but the years and changing taste had contrived to kiss it and its

5

genteel elegance goodbye. New skyscrapers now busted the Los Angeles skyline downtown, and in their wake they brought huge glass-and-chromium high rises from the big international hotel chains. They got the new business while the old Marrot got the spill and the shaft. It was called progress, another fact of life that brooked no argument.

A lot of colorfully dressed people were jamming the sidewalks outside. Body freaks, boy and girl groupies milling around, while strong-armed body-builder types leaned against the building, arms folded on their chests, watching for some action. Customized cars rubbed bumpers with classy sports jobs along the curb. There was a festive holiday spirit prevailing, with sidewalk merchants doing a brisk business and the blue-coated guardians of the law looking the other way and keeping the traffic moving.

Suddenly the old building seemed to rock with a noisy madness, a tumultuous beating sound of applause accented by moaning cries. You get this from the rapt body crowds just as you do at the football and baseball games, only the keening, moaning noises are particular to the body-building events.

I moved past a pack of kids blocking the door. One of them spit nastily at my feet. "No sweat, man. It's only prejudging time."

I nodded and moved through the door. A prejudging in body building is the whole ball game; it's the contest. The rest of it later is spread out to titillate the crowds, making it a show where the results have already been decided by the prejudging the morning or afternoon before. Prejudging takes care of the technical part, like the school figures necessary in skating-competition events.

Except for the Mr. Olympia, which has no divisions, all International Federation of Body Builders contests use the prejudging to divide the contestants into three height classes. Class One is for the short men, under five feet five; next are the mediums, between five-five and five-eight; and finally the tall men, over five-eight. Up to six places are picked in each height category. The overall winner is selected from the three class winners.

The short class is taken on first by the judges, followed by the mediums and the talls, ending in the final pose-down between the three class winners for the overall championship title. The big guys seem to have it all, but sometimes they are knocked off by a shorter man who can put it all together better, and show it with the right kind of expertise and flair. It's more than parading the beef; you have to know how to sell it. The moaning, applauding, cheering crowd reacting to the brief muscular dance of the body builder gets to the judges, letting them know the man the crowd wants to win it.

I followed the limp yucca plants and the peeling paint across the hotel lobby. The once-plush furniture, rugs and draperies that had entertained royalty and bigwigs were faded now, as depressing as a dowager who won't quit. The clerks sat behind their counters dreaming of better days. A glass directory had the Mr. Universe contest spelled out. I followed the moaning, ecstatic cries up the frayed carpeting, past the chipped statuary, to the ballroom on the mezzanine floor called the Florentine Room.

A well-stacked little bunny was swapping tickets for money outside the glass doors leading to the large ballroom. She had seen them all and looked me over without buckling her dimpled knees. There had to be at least fifty guys inside who could beat out the rest of the world, another hundred or so in the audience good enough to win local contests. There was no way ordinary people could score here.

The hot September afternoon had already wilted some of the beefy bodies inside, crowded shoulder to shoulder, flank to flank, on wooden chairs. There were a lot of cute chicks alone or with their own muscle men. A lot of big gals, smiling, sweating and yelling. The gay ones were there, too, along with the other sexes.

Down front was the raised stage and the long table of the judges, twenty feet from where the competitors stood. The body builders milled around dressed in their own weird threads, each carrying his own little gym bag with towel, trunks and body oil, looking at each other impassively, trying not to be psyched out.

7

The fans included housewives, workers, L.A. citizens and out-of-towners, rapists, voyeurs, pimps, perverts, straights, agents, businessmen, health nuts, iron freaks and college kids. The real people. All very involved in the narcissist world of the weight men and body builders, their flesh idols, all assembled now under one roof, the best developed, most beautiful male bodies in the universe.

Long tables near the entrance were covered with circulars and health-food products. They carried pictures and endorsements of the body-building champs. Nobody said he owed it all to steroids, or got into the torture of lifting mind-boggling totals of tons of iron regularly every day for at least ten years. The long hard hours of sweating and killing your body trying to make it number one, the king of the world.

Instead the accent was on the food boosters, the powerizers, protozymes, Insta-Power drinks, natural-organic Energex tablets, superproteins, Yoga-Tone wafers, high-potency weight-plus iron scientifically blended with bromelain, wheat-germ oil, B 12 and papaya. Becoming number one in the iron freaking sport takes more sustained pain, struggle and motivation than any other. But the ad men wanted you to know it was the product, those little things in the jars and bottles that would do it all for you.

Down front some men were signing in, being measured for their height and weight. Others were already backstage (called the pit) after being classified, in their skimpy posing trunks, oiling up their bodies, then pumping themselves up. They try to get all the blood into their muscles for the bulk they want to impress the judges.

The first round for each height category is nonscoring. A prelim round. Judges watching as the contestants parade around, making notes on their half-dozen work sheets. Each height class comes out again as a group for the second round. They give the judges front, back and side views without flexing or posing. At this stage the judges are looking for symmetry, general appearance and proportion. The muscularity bit comes later.

8

In the third and final round, the body builders have ninety seconds to do a routine of the compulsory and optional poses. The six compulsory ones come first. Double-biceps from the front, abdominals flexed. Front lat flex with flexed legs. Right side-biceps and shoulder with the side of the leg flexed. Back double-biceps. Rear lat spread with both calves flexed. A left side pose with triceps, chest and left leg flexed. These are the pure poses in body building and there's no way a man can cheat.

After the scoring, totals are added. Each competitor gets marked from 1 to 20. The three winners—short, medium and tall—are then brought out again. They'll do the same poses side by side until the overall winner is chosen. This is the one-minute classic pose-off, the one they sweat and strain their guts out for all year. Now they have to put it all together, hit with their best, lay it out with all their power and controlled grace. The fans scream in ecstasy as the overhead lights pick out the muscled cuts and definitions of the powerful oiled bodies.

The body builders are like hams at this point, sensing what the crowd wants, dramatically putting out their galvanized choreography in isolated shots, pinpointing their best attributes. They have to be flexible in their routine, cutting when the applause falls, hitting and holding longer when they sense rapport with the screamers wanting more of this or that.

The aficionados know the poses, what's coming and who owned it—Corney, Katz, Schwarzenegger, Scott, Sergio, Leon Brown—and root, moan, groan and heckle like fans in other sports. At their loudest, the din is rhythmic, frenzied, unimaginable. And they can chill a contestant's chances just as fast with a negative silence as they can boost him in with cheers.

The judges begin looking for overall size and shape, body structure and skin tone. Then they look closer at the muscle groups, note how they relate. They take in the neck and face muscles, sometimes even rate the jawline for contour. They're looking at the trapezius muscles behind the shoulder area for width and slope, the thick twin bulk of muscles that cradles the back of the head. The deltoids—for separation of the three sheaths. The pectoralis merging with the anterior deltoids on the chest. They judge the sternum, and the upper and lower grooves of muscle dividing it.

On the arm flex they like clear-cut divisions between the bicep two heads and the three deltoids. They look for the furrowed iliac, the segmented turtlelike carapace in the *linea alba* of the stomach. They look at the outer shape of the latissimus dorsi for the taper effect. They check the obliques and serratus, the small thick chunks of muscle linking the lats and rib cage. They flex for the trapezius, deltoids, *infraspinatus* and erector muscles. They check the legs for the frontal thighs, the deepness of the quadriceps, the definition of the *peroneus longus*, the sartorius, the diamond shape of the calf muscle.

They look at the feet. The Achilles tendons. The forearms, skin, striation of muscles. Then they sit back as the man tries to snap it all together with dramatic transitions in the souped-up choreography of his body. I've been around when a man fails. The chump is so tired from pumping himself up in the pit that by the time his name is called, he can't lift his arms. Or he goes into cramps, muscle spasms, and has to be helped off.

The man at the mike was reciting the available awards. First prize for best abdominals, or chest, arms or back. Best legs, best lats—best anything a man had. Size was not too important here, and the small men stood a chance. Some already had the minor wins, the sectional or regional championships, good for a year of plugs in the health and strength mags, tie-ins with health-product producers. A lot of freeloading and the acquisition of a minor bunny stable down at Muscle Beach.

The crowd wasn't listening. The big win this night would be getting crowned Mr. Universe. The winner could run his take up to over fifty grand a year, plus all the product he could eat. Maybe he would get a shot at a film where they needed that kind of beefy body beautiful to help some B picture along. Certainly the winner had it made with the chicks and could help himself to all the beautiful cuddly muscle-struck blond, brunette and Titian-tressed little birds all over this world.

I walked down the aisle, out the side door, and cut across to the pit, the backstage dressing rooms. The door was open and I saw a lot of near-naked men, in skimpy trunks, flexing their muscles. If the air conditioning was on, it was fighting a losing battle with the sweat pouring from their glistening bodies. Some had already applied their body oil, others were just shining with perspiration, breathing hard, working their arms, pumping their blood and themselves up.

Nobody minded my rubbernecking. Body builders live on attentive awe. There were all colors, shapes and sizes. Short-haired, long-haired, clean-shaven, bearded and mustachioed. All were impressively developed. Muscles wriggled and writhed like snakes. Some men were very small and looked grotesque with more muscle on them than they could decently handle. There were legs like fire hydrants, abdominals like washboards, necks no shirtmaker could ever hope to collar. Several with outsize pectoral development had more going for them than some of the cuties in a Vegas line.

The body-sweat stench was overpowering and I walked away. Felix Witter could have been there, somewhere in the back, behind those broad bodies and thick slatted shoulders, but I didn't see him. His group, the bigger men, would be the last to be called. Not too many champs duck into the ring first, preferring to let the challenger worry and cool off waiting.

The bar downstairs was cooler, and a couple of drinks got my mind off the zoo parade upstairs. It had better air circulating, too. I stayed with the booze and ice in the glass until I thought it was time to take in the body show.

I heard titters when I came through the door. There was piped music, and some oversized Adonis was mincing across the stage, flexing and unflexing his muscles in time to the canned tune. He stopped, did his regular figures, turned profile and showed his beautiful belly, then backside, stooped, swerved, threw his head back, froze, articulated his muscles, held his definition, relaxed, bowed gracefully. The tune ended while he was trying for one more extended profile view. He walked off pouting.

He drew some half-hearted applause, a few catcalls. More women were edging into the audience. Sensational-looking chicks wearing very little to show their own ideas about body

11

building. The beefy oversized Amazons, the kind who work out at the gals' side of the gym, strong enough to be full-time bouncers. Either way you looked at them, they could knock your eye out.

Number 49 came out, chunky and muscular, thick-chested, walking with his arms bent, his lats stretched to make him look more massive. He flexed arms that weren't any bigger than telephone poles. A wise-apple kid applauded wildly. The poser frowned. He turned, took a deep breath, closed his eyes and exhaled slowly. He opened his eyes and was surprised to see his arms still hanging out there. He tried again. He wanted to try a double-biceps from the front with the abdominals flexed. His arms cramped and he had to stop and shake them loose. This time they dropped. The audience cheered and he walked off muttering to himself, drawing more cheers and razzing sounds.

I remembered an office call I had to make and stepped on a few toes moving down the row. The telephone call gave me more bad news. A big shipment we were casing got away. An agent was shot. Mr. Big was punching holes in our line. I hit the bar again with a double Scotch. I nursed it, along with my depression, hoping for the wheels inside my head to track me onto something. They were stuck and wouldn't turn over. I tossed some money on the pocked wood bar and went up again to see the muscle show.

I'd waited a shade too long. The ballroom was hushed. Heads turned and angry faces looked up at me as I muscled my way across a row of bodies to a rear seat off the aisle. Felix Witter was walking barefoot across the stage.

His freshly oiled body glistened and sparkled under the bright overhead lights. His incredible development brought startled sounds from those in the audience who had never seen what a lifetime dedicated to body building could do for a very determined man. Girls stared unbelievingly at his superstructure, this beautiful, gorgeous hunk of man. Men goggled, too, popeyed in disbelief, shaking their heads at his awesome musculature.

Witter didn't need music. His own body was a symphony

enveloping his movement. He smiled tolerantly at the excited "oohs" and "aahs." He had heard them before. He stopped and faced the audience, raised and flexed his outsize arms. They were easily double the size of the ordinary male's, and the crowd gasped as if in shock. He turned to display his broad back with arms raised. The incredibly wide thick line of his latissimus dorsi flowing under the broad triangle of the trapezius, from shoulders to waist, was inhumanly broad. His upper body swelled hugely with the girth of two men coupled, mighty and massive—a towering construction of thick muscle bulking and flaring over the disproportionately small midsection.

The audience applauded what had to be the most architecturally developed male body ever displayed. Felix Witter was undoubtedly at first sight Mr. America, Mr. World, Mr. Universe, Mr. Olympia—the all-time champion of the only sport a man can wear.

He held his pose, his arms high, and flexed a moment longer. A ripple started in his upper back, rolled across his spine. His huge biceps twitched. His "lats" fluttered. Was he cramping? Somebody in the audience laughed nervously. Witter turned his head. His face was red and he looked embarrassed. He shrugged his wide shoulders. His pectoral muscles jiggled and jumped under his skin. He bit his lip, frowning.

His nose twitched now and he dropped his arms as if they had suddenly become too heavy. He slapped almost angrily at his chest to stop the fluttering, uncontrollable muscle. Under that glistening skin, little clusters of muscle began to vibrate, doing their own devilish dance. There were titters from the audience.

Witter rubbed at his chest. His hand soothed away the ripples. He twisted his head and rubbed at his throat. He seemed to have trouble breathing. His chest heaved and his face became redder. He looked toward the judges at their table, his eyes rolling in silent apology. He shook his blond thatch of hair, took a deep breath and didn't like it. He began to claw at his throat again now, his lips moving in a silent plea. The muscles locked on his upper arm and he tried to slap the cramp away.

Now his thigh muscles began to twitch and jiggle. It was like a giant network of electrical impulses suddenly gone berserk. Witter froze, seemingly afraid to move. The audience laughed.

Witter turned profile. His chest heaved again as he tried sucking air. His face reddened more and he shook his head in distress, apparently unable to exhale or get oxygen into his lungs. He opened his mouth and made a gasping sound, tried to speak, and then toppled to the stage floor, coming down stiffly like a giant felled oak.

He hit the floor hard. The audience was on its feet now and I was trying to get down the aisle, but there were too many already there, trying to reach him. Seats were smashed over, men and women knocked aside as the burlier men moved forward. Women screamed, picked themselves off the floor and were knocked aside again.

By the time I got there, they had carried him into the back room. But he was already out of the Mr. Universe contest and on his way to another arena where people go after they die.

Two

Doc Shipman was the medical examiner for Homicide West Los Angeles. Doing inventories over dead bodies for twenty years hadn't done any more for his naturally dour disposition than you would expect. He watched me come in without forcing his seamed face into a smile. He lit a dead stogie instead and waved the acrid smoke away.

"About Felix Witter," I said, "I was there watching him do his thing."

Shipman wagged his head. "No accounting, I suppose. But I thought you went more for girls."

"Offhand, I don't know any girls worth killing, Doc. What happened to Superman?"

Shipman grunted. "You were there, Roper. You were a witness. You're supposed to be some kind of a detective. What do you think happened?"

"I think somebody wanted him dead. I'm here to find out how it was done."

The dour ME grunted and opened a desk drawer. He lifted a small plastic bottle with a screw-on cap. "We found this in Witter's gym bag. I imagine he thought it was his usual rubbing oil that he was applying to his body before posing."

He unscrewed the top and let me have my whiff. It was pungent and unpleasant, like any other liniment rubbing oil. He put the cap back and held the bottle to the light. Tiny flecks stirred and settled back in the viscous contents.

I rubbed my nose. I remembered the heat and strong body odors in the backstage dressing room. The added smells of the various liniments, rubdown lotions, oils and pomades. The more natural concomitant ones of fear and anxiety.

"Okay," I said, "it's strong stuff, but nobody could smell anything in that room worse than the guy standing next to him. I can't imagine him taking even a little nip of the stuff. How did it kill him?"

Shipman favored me with a forensic smile. He picked up a book labeled *Poisons*. A card was inserted at a chapter listing pesticides, the "economic poisons." I opened the book and read the top killers in the groups of substances used in man's relentless war on his ubiquitous enemies. Insecticides, fungicides, herbicides, rodenticides and ascaricides.

Shipman nodded and took back his book. "It's any one in that group and we haven't decided which, yet. Acute poisoning occurs after inhalation or when contact with the skin has been made. We can assume both occurred with the deceased."

"His muscles were jumping out of control, then going into spasm before he showed trouble breathing."

The ME shrugged. "There's an enzyme known as cholinesterase. When the autonomic nervous system is poisoned, the enzyme is blocked and an accumulation of acetylcholine takes place. This stimulates and later paralyzes all nerve synapses and motor nerve endings."

I picked up the bottle and held it to the light. The little flecks stirred and moved slowly and settled back. "What about those little bright flecks?"

"Something added to complete the job. Gold dust. Covered the pores completely. Witter, already in trouble with the poison on his skin, couldn't breathe it out. He would have been experiencing disturbed vision, disorientation, convulsions leading to coma. Stated simply, Witter became toxic to the vapors. His breathing apparatus failed. I'm writing it up as death due to strangulation with consequent heart failure. Any questions?"

16

I fiddled with the cap. "I'd like another sniff, Doc."

Doc Shipman took it out of my hand and put the plastic death dealer back in his desk drawer. "Suicide isn't your bag, Roper. Go out and find the killer."

"That's a job for Lieutenant Camino and the police. I've enough on my back trying to track down some wise apple in narcotics who's killing us. Getting back to Witter, that man was too big and strong to get a heart attack and die that fast. You're sure it's just the body rubbing oil with the added insecticide?"

Doc Shipman scratched his ear. "I hear you but I don't believe you're saying it. What difference does it make how big and strong you are if you can't breathe? How long can you last—three minutes? Five with superior lung capacity? He could have died from heat prostration and anxiety. You buy that?"

"I'll go along with your topical poisoning theory. But I'll wait for your final autopsy report."

Shipman frowned. "Why haggle over details? The guy was young, big, stronger than a bull, with more muscles than I was told about in med school. He's still dead."

I looked carefully at the police surgeon. "What's come over you? You never care about what your meat wagon delivers. A stiff is always a stiff to you."

"Right," he said. "I need this job, you understand? It helps me meet people. Even if they're dead."

I stared, puzzled. "What are you trying to tell me?"

He shrugged, sad-eyed and uncomfortable. "Life is funny. It has surprising twists. Have you ever noticed?"

"I haven't had the time," I said. "I spend too much of it listening to old forensic experts beating around the bush."

He sighed and blew his nose. "It just so happens, a niece of mine was going with this fellow. What's his name?"

"Felix Witter. What's the name of your niece?"

"It took you long enough to ask," Doc Shipman said.

Three

She was young, had long black hair and was wearing a short yellow dress. Good healthy figure. Prettier than a coroner's niece could be.

I addressed deep-blue, untroubled eyes. "Miss Debbie Hill?"

"Yes?" She held the door. Symptom of the times.

"My name is Roper. Doc Shipman suggested that I see you."

"Why?" Saying his name didn't make her open the door wider.

"I'm a detective. Your uncle said you had a relationship going with Felix Witter."

She tossed her long hair, unimpressed by family gossip. "Look around, mister. You'll find I wasn't the only one."

"A Mr. Universe tends to attract lots of pretty girls," I said. "I thought you would be concerned about his murder."

Her eyes widened, her full red lips parted, her high curved chest rose and she gulped air. I had found a magic word or two to set her system off to doing things. "Murder?" she said, almost angrily. "Who said anything about his being murdered?"

"Your uncle Shipman, the local police pathologist, medical examiner, and reigning forensic authority of L.A. Homicide West. I thought you knew about it."

"I just got in from out of town. I heard about Felix on TV. There wasn't anything said about murder." She looked into my steely eyes. "Hey, am I supposed to be a suspect?"

I smiled. "If you are, you'll be the first. May I come inside?"

She thought about it. "I suppose you have some kind of identification? Uncle Marvin knows a lot of strange people."

I flashed the billfold with buzzer over the small type. She leaned closer to take it all in. She smelled fresh and sweet and I restrained a sudden urge to nibble on her ear. She looked up suddenly as if divining the thought and smiled. "All right, Mr. Roper. I suppose talking won't hurt."

I followed her inside and waited while she went around putting on lights. "I just took this apartment. I didn't realize it was so dark when I signed the lease."

"Seems like you've been doing a lot of things lately," I said. "Where were you living before?"

"San Francisco. But I've had it up there. It's too cold."

"What about all those nice warm restaurants for taking off the chill?"

She sat down opposite me, doing it gracefully, showing me she had nicely contoured long slim legs. "I'm afraid I haven't seen too much of them," she said, almost apologetically. "Maybe that was another reason for moving down to L.A."

It never makes sense when the lovely ones own up to a hungering loneliness. This one should have been lined up for every hour in the day, but then, you never know what goes on inside.

"Tell me about you and Felix Witter. It shouldn't be too difficult. Unless you happen to be a great actress, you don't appear to be grieving."

She nodded gravely, accepting the line without anger. "Maybe a few months ago, I might have been grieving. After finding out a lot more about him than I knew, it wasn't that difficult to forget I ever knew him."

I waved my hands. "You should have told your uncle. He thinks you're desolate and you won't be whole again or happy until I come up with Witter's killer."

She smiled. "I'll call him and set him straight about it. I really can't blame him because the last time I spoke with Uncle

Marvin I was head over heels in love with that—that"—she snapped her fingers at me—"give me a word."

"Fellow." I said.

"With that bastard."

I sat back. I took out my little black memo book and a pen. "Just the relevant facts. Like, why was he a bastard and what brought it all on, and so forth, Miss Hill? You don't have to speak slowly. I can't read my notes, anyway."

She nodded and pulled her short skirt down toward her smooth rounded knees. I had to appreciate each moment because I knew after her I could be interviewing a lot of ugly husky men with bulging thighs, blown-up arms, short necks and most likely shorter tempers.

"I'm in the health-food business," she said. "A West Coast chain of stores called Good Earth Things. I'm a nutritionist and salesperson. I also do promotion, publicity, anything to help move the product. That includes a lot of lectures on health to interested groups, and means a good deal of traveling."

I nodded. "And that's how you—"

She cut in, as salespersons tend to do these days. "I met Felix Witter at a health-food convention in San Francisco. The vitamin sales group was there, the natural and organic products —and the other people hustling their own thing related to the field. Felix Witter was representing his high-protein products, the ones he endorsed publicly. Naturally, with his incredible physical appearance he tended to dominate the affair, and his being top man in the body-building contests all over the world didn't hurt him either. We were introduced. He stayed in town long enough for us to get to know each other"—she clasped and looked down at her hands—"it was kind of sudden, I'm afraid."

I made little reassuring hand motions. "It happens. Any man with Witter's build could overwhelm almost any salesperson, or for that matter, any woman he set his sights for. Actually, the important thing is—"

She didn't go along with other people finishing sentences. "The immediate result was that I sent in a whopping big order for his health-supplement product—my largest ever. I lost my head trying to hold his interest, I suppose. The owner questioned my judgment, asked if people were dying suddenly for lack of Witter's High-Protein wafer. We have a large chain of stores in the state, but still, you only buy what you can move off the shelf. And then there was a big delay in getting it. Felix said the manufacturer couldn't keep up with the demand."

"But you weren't stiffed—the product did arrive?" She nodded, and I said, "Then what—?"

"The shipment came after a long delay, but fortunately the product proved to be a fast-moving item, perhaps because of Witter's association with it. In any event, nobody was hurt."

She stopped and looked at me for another question or comment she could interrupt. I couldn't think of any. She decided at last to go it alone again.

"Felix traveled as front man for his product, along with a lot of other sidelines he was merchandising. We saw a great deal of each other when he was in the San Francisco area. When he was scheduled at nearby cities, I sometimes arranged my own schedule to coincide with his." She looked intently at me. "I had a crush on him, I suppose. Any girl in sight went ga-ga over him, not to mention a lot of men."

"I'm glad you brought that last bit up, Miss Hill," I said. "Because I was wondering—"

Her blue eyes blazed cold flame and chilled my mouth shut. "Naturally, I was more concerned about all those women—you might call them health-food groupies—and I didn't take the faggoty men seriously as any kind of threat."

I ventured again, cautiously. "Did Felix swing both ways, perhaps?" She stared. "Maybe you want me to explain that?"

Her crossed leg swung an attractive petulant arc. "It doesn't matter now, does it? He's dead, anyway, and I'm over being a fool about the situation."

I forced my eyes away from that attractively contoured swinging leg down to the blank spaces in my open memo book. "Maybe we could take it from the point of your falling out," I suggested. "Sometimes that can—"

Her voice came over mine quickly, softer, her face dreamy. "It didn't take too long, really. I had already made rather a fool of myself with repeated large orders of his damn milk-and-cellulose wafers. My boss called several times to check my sanity. But I was able to point out the risk was negligible, that Felix Witter was a very big name in the muscle world, and so on, and got away with it. I was insane, of course, out of my head for fear of losing him, and when you're in love, you do foolish, unpredictable things."

I tried to remember the last time I was in love. Memory had dimmed the trail and provided instead more recent examples of an erratic mind confusedly at work without benefit of being star-kissed.

"No question about it," I said warmly, "love can do some funny things. Definitely affects the mind, and so forth. Now, when was the last time you saw Felix Witter? I suppose that can end this interview. Unless you happen to know of some people who didn't particularly like him. For reasons other than yours, of course."

She tossed back her long soft hair with a quick headshake, and then played a tune on its edges with pliant fingers. "The last time I saw him was two months ago. He was down here in L.A. and I went to see him in his hotel room."

I waited patiently, having heard of other girls visiting other men in their hotel rooms.

"It was the kind of trip I could account for—business reasons—we have store outlets here, too. But I had been changing my schedule since I met him, always inventing different reasons. Anyway, the point is, I found evidence of another woman having been there with him shortly before I arrived—and he knew I was coming."

She looked embarrassed. I smiled encouragingly. "You have to remember these superman types aren't like us ordinary mortals. They're bigger and stronger and have larger appetites."

She threw her head back and laughed. She stopped laughing and said, "That's really a crock," and went right back into her last peal of laughter.

I shrugged and adjusted my collar. It wasn't my business to

defend or vouch for supermen. "Okay," I said, "so we've disposed of the folklore. He wasn't all that hot in the sack." I wanted to add that perhaps Mr. Witter had generally managed to have had his way with a gaggle of other nubile and willing maidens before she arrived on other occasions, too, but decided to stay on safer ground. "Muscles don't always mean performance, not in that category, anyway. Now, did you ever see Felix Witter after that argument?"

"What argument?"

I sighed. "The one in his hotel room after you found the indisputable evidence of his having had another woman before you—"

She giggled. She had nice white teeth that undoubtedly would be punched out one day unless she changed her ways with interrogators. "Oh, we didn't quarrel over that," she said. "I knew at that instant that I would be stupid not to expect the same thing happening over and over again, at any time and any travel point in Felix Witter's life. So I made up my mind that I would cut the monkey rope and not ever see him again."

"You told him that—then?"

"Well, yes . . . afterward, I mean."

"How did he take it?"

"Rather badly, to tell the truth. What I didn't realize at the time was that Felix was a very jealous man."

I looked my puzzled best.

"He knew I was seeing some innocuous little college assistant professor in San Francisco. He demanded that I stop seeing Freddie and of course I told him—"

I had my notebook close, pen hand at the ready. "Freddie who?"

"Freddie Guest. He's at Berkeley—biochemistry, physiology, body-brain biofeedback, that scene."

I made the notations fast. "Okay. So Witter was jealous and you argued, I suppose. Did you have any other friends Mr. Witter might have had similar feelings about? Jealousy does funny things to people too, Miss Hill. It's nearly as funny as being in love."

She thought about it. She pushed the edges of her skirt down a millimeter and looked at her fingernails. They looked red and well-polished.

"Well," she said, "I don't want to give you the wrong impression. Especially since you know my uncle. But actually, I know quite a large number of these men."

"College professors? Biochemists?" Biochemists could easily know more than the average would-be killer about toxic drugs and poisons.

She shook her head. "No, the muscle men. The weight lifters and body builders like Felix. In the health-food business, you meet an awful lot of them associated with product promotion, like Felix Witter was."

My hand hung over the memo book but I had a sudden sick feeling I might not have enough pages. "Perhaps you could name some," I said. "Just so I'll have something to work with."

Her pert nose wrinkled. "Oh, nobody special, you understand. Most of them are or were champions, like Mr. America, Mr. Universe, Mr. West Coast, Mr. California, Mr. San Diego— most of them are hustling something, you know, and naturally I knew them from the same kind of health-food promotion affairs."

I forced a cagey smile. "So Felix Witter wasn't the only muscle man in your life?"

"I don't know what that's supposed to mean exactly," she said. "I know weight lifters, body builders, gymnasts, boxers, wrestlers, a lot of jocks. People are taking their health seriously these days." She leaned toward me appraisingly. "Do you take vitamin supplements, Mr. Roper?"

"Not yet. Booze keeps me going."

"Whiskey depletes your vitamin B reserves," she said. "If you drink a lot, you should add a high-potency B-complex vitamin to your diet."

"It would be easier if the brewers put it into the bottle. Now, about these muscle men. . . ."

She smiled. "I don't mean to give you the impression that I'm putting it all down to the nature of my business. I think I've always been attracted to big strong-looking men."

I sucked in my gut, sat forward. "A lot of them around," I said. "Do you know any who wanted Felix Witter dead?"

"No, not actually. But he wasn't well-liked. He never cared about that. He walked over people, eroded them, acted as if they didn't exist. If you ask around, you might find a hundred suspects."

"It's not my case," I said. "As long as you're clear, I'm out of it. If you tell me you didn't kill Witter, I'll take your word for it and tell your uncle not to worry. If you change your mind, and remember suddenly that you did kill him, let me know so we could set up a reasonable defense."

"I don't remember killing him," she said. "Is that enough for you to go on?"

"Absolutely. I'm only a private dick. I can afford to be more reasonable than the LAPD." She got up and pulled down her little skirt. I pushed myself out of the seat. "You did say the last time you saw Felix Witter was two months ago?"

"Yes."

"And you don't recall switching a poisonous rubdown oil somehow before the Mr. Universe contest for the one he normally used?"

Her eyes stayed on mine. "No. Is that how it was done?"

"According to your uncle, the medical examiner, it was."

She frowned. "How could that kill him—what was it?"

"An insecticide on his skin that paralyzed his breathing apparatus and he strangled to death. Maybe a rat poison."

She nodded. "The killer must have known Felix well." As I went past her to the door, she said, "Remember to add more vitamin B to your diet. It's very good for your nerves."

She opened the door, not giving way too much, and I brushed past her. Sometimes you get so wrapped up chasing killers, you forget how nice girls can smell. The door closed behind me and I went down the steps and along the walk. As I neared the street, a man slipped sideways out of his parked car. He came up the walk and I got a better look at him front view. His chest and biceps bulged out of his thin short-sleeved sport shirt. He was massive, dark and good-looking.

He flashed a friendly grin showing big white choppers. "Hi, Debbie in?"

I wagged my thumb over my shoulder. "You're next."

He nodded happily. As we passed on the narrow walk, our shoulders touched. His didn't feel any harder than granite. I turned to take another look at him. He wasn't as big as Felix Witter, but big enough. I had seen his pictures in the health and strength magazines.

Eddie Blue. Former Mr. America, one-time Mr. World and twice Mr. Universe. A man with a reputedly great track record for scoring with the chicks. I could understand his happy smile as he walked up to Debbie Hill's apartment. With Felix Witter out of it, the competition was going to be easier in a lot of different events.

Four

I drove away from the swinging singles Marina del Rey part of town thinking about its current leaseholder Debbie Hill, nutritionist and salesperson. A lot of chicks like their men wide-shouldered and virile-looking, along with muscles and the brute energy they convey. I pictured her with Felix Witter, and now with Eddie Blue. She knew nearly all the muscle men, she had said, and after Blue there were still plenty available, an ever-expanding crop of young and powerful iron men, along with the current stand-bys. The panorama became too intense, and I shook my head and tried remembering Debbie Hill at her worst. A nagging nutritionist feminist who would remind a guy to stock up on his vitamins instead of kissing him goodbye.

I headed the heap into the downtown lot behind the EPT offices, and went up the side stairs. The offices are a series of interlocking rooms with a dummy front presided over by some respectable-looking old ladies. The listing on the lobby register is E-Z Percussion Tools, but nobody buys any. Backstage is the operating core of O. J. Burr's espionage and detection service. EPT means Emergency Procedure Terminus. You call Burr and EPT when you have nowhere else to go.

Burr is a lanky bristle-headed master of intrigue. Once a history prof, he went into the Big War working for the OSS and came into his own as a genius at counterdeceit. Later he joined

27

the top secret ops in Washington. But he was too much his own man to put up with shenanigans he disagreed with, left and started running his own operation on the West Coast. He collected a good tight group of experienced agents and dicks like myself willing to work Burr's way, the tidy way. He sells his services to people with problems they can't solve themselves. Lately he seems to have taken on the world for his playground.

The current big play was the drug scene, always tough, hydra-headed, springing up seemingly renewed and stronger whenever you thought you had it put down and away. Los Angeles was becoming the spin-off for the nation's clearing house for illegal dope distribution, San Francisco.

The Golden Gate area is the top international port of entry, the stuff coming in from faraway places. Peru, Bangkok, Mexico City, Bolivia. The Golden Triangle of Burma, Laos and Cambodia, where the poppies grown on mountaintops in unpopulated areas are outside governmental jurisdicton. Marijuana comes in from Tijuana along with brown Mexican heroin. Cocaine from Rio de Janeiro and Bolivia in little plastic bags the runners sometimes have taped to their thighs and chests. The East Coast cities have been replaced as the heroin hub by our town, L.A. It's the heroin capital of the world, and with twenty-four little bags selling for $10 million, business is very good.

There are at least a thousand major drug figures operating in Northern California alone, the men who finance the overall operation. Young men, out to make a big bundle, and maybe then go into legit business. They can start out small, selling the small package of heroin, four pounds for a quarter of a million on the street, and they're on their way. Pure cocaine will net $2 million for about eight pounds. Either way, they get rich fast.

Young men are more daring and energetic than the older ones; their dreams are infinite, their imagination rarefied. Because of all this recklessness and vitality unleashed in their drives toward their personal goals, they can be trouble, a considerable pain in the butt to deal with.

What they're going for, is their slice of the world. The power that goes with it, along with the easy life and the broads, the big houses, cars, boats, Riviera style. The continental pickings get you more for the dollar. They come in all shapes and descriptions, from all levels of society, and can't be programed or made to fit any calculable mold. They're just out there somewhere doing their thing, thumbing their noses at you and the various constrictions of the law, telling you to go screw and try to get them.

We were running with special task forces this trip: agents of the Drug Enforcement Administration; the FBI; the Internal Revenue Service, Alcohol, Firearms and Tobacco Division; and local nark agents and police. A few agents had dropped but so far they belonged to the other guys. When I checked in, I found out that one of ours, agent Dill SW 2, was missing.

Other than the code name, Dill was Bradshaw. Red-headed, dogged, a taut wiry man with a nose for skullduggery and an eye for the women, both factors contriving to keep him at a continuing high tension. He was working the San Francisco drug scene with the state task force narcotic agents, and seemingly the spoor had led him back to L.A.

Missing didn't mean dead necessarily, but missing too long would cinch the betting and change the odds on Bradshaw's breathing again. Working for O. J. Burr can get you killed in many different ways, a lot of them time-consuming and dangerous before you get boxed in. The original challenge and bright purpose that first sucked us in had worn thin with time and flaked with the residues of fear and tough bargaining. We knew now the game was on and would never end, the goal posts were crooked, as was the referee, the stakes were against us and running higher. A sensible betting man would have turned in his card and walked away, but after too many years you forget the meaning of being sensible.

You can't put down the education, and as in traveling, you get to meet a lot of interesting people. Sometimes these people stomp on you and try to kick your brains loose. Other times you get in your own licks. And then there are the more pleasurable aspects. One happens to be on hand in our outfit, a little heaven

29

in the flesh, well-rounded, right-sized, with a grace, beauty and totally ingenuous nonchalance that makes all the gung-hoing plausible. Our own office girl and secretary, Miss Sarah Troy.

With a tinkly little-girl voice coming out of all this wondrous femininity, one's erotic fantasies are oddly stimulated. As a famous mind mechanic once said, one fact alone means little, but when there are others, you must sit up and take notice. And the proven fact downtown at the EPT hangout for dicks and derring-doers is that Miss Troy can set a grown man's jaw to slavering faster than a two-pound sizzling tenderloin.

I pulled in my gut as usual when passing this delectable bit of fluff, raised my chest and nodded winningly in her general direction. And as usual Miss Troy kept her seat without crossing her beautiful legs, hiking her skirt, pushing back her hair or giving any other overt body signs of a faster heartbeat at my appearance.

"A message about agent Dill, Mr. Roper. I put it on your desk."

"I'll get right to it, Miss Troy. Anything else?"

The cornflower-blue eyes regarded me distinctly. "No, sir."

"No lovely helpless damsels fearing the clutch of jealous swain asking for my protective arm?"

"Oh no, sir."

"No wealthy tycoon's daughter, beautiful and teen-aged, abducted and held for ransom, needing my immediate pursuit with extra per diem for traveling expenses?"

She blinked in three-quarter time. "I thought we already did that last month."

I had put that one behind me. The wealthy tycoon's daughter, as it turned out, had helped to abduct herself, party to a scheme to screw her old man for purposes of a new life with an exciting lover, hooked on drugs and imaginative ways of insuring a lifetime supply.

"True, Miss Troy," I said. "Well then, perhaps you're not doing anything special this evening and we could—"

The teeny tinkly little-girl voice made smiling tolerant sounds. "Oh, Mr. Roper—you're never serious."

30

I went to my inner office to get serious. The message about agent Dill was from a state undercover nark agent named Parson. He reported seeing our man Dill twelve hours earlier establishing contact with a man and a woman. Twelve hours prior to that time was the last we had heard from Dill. He could have been arranging a sale and bust, and been hit himself.

I knew Parson slightly, didn't like him. Big, tough and sadistic, the kind who leans on the cripples. His message puzzled me for a number of reasons. The phone rang. I said hello.

"Parson here. Get my message?"

"Right. Can you give us anything to go on?"

Parson breathed heavily. "Look, forget Dill. I saw him punched out, dragged to a car."

"When? Give me a make on the car."

"It was a green—"

There was a muffled coughing sound I didn't like. Parson probably wasn't happy about it either. The line went dead. I jiggled the cradle, hit the button, got Miss Troy at the board outside.

"Stay with that call. Keep the line open."

"I'll try. Meanwhile, another message came in while you were talking."

"Let's have it."

"I'd better bring it in."

She came in seconds later, a tiny crease between her brows, and handed me the message. "I'd swear it was him talking."

The message was brief and cryptic. DANTE'S DYNASTY SUNSET SNOWFALL.

I looked up at Miss Troy, hanging nervously over my desk. "You didn't say who called this in."

She took a deep breath. "Agent Dill. That's what puzzled me because I heard"—she exhaled, but her chest still looked full and interesting—"Mr. Parson. I thought he was dead."

I shrugged. "Maybe they're both dead. Meanwhile, get back to your board and see if they've anything on Parson, and where he was calling from."

She slipped out and I concentrated on the message. I checked the phone directory. "Dante's Dynasty" was a hair salon for men. In Hollywood off Sunset Boulevard. "Snow" is nark talk for cocaine; "snowfall" could mean it was drifting into or through Dante's Dynasty, unless agent Dill was talking about dandruff, and I couldn't imagine why. "Sunset" suggested an after-dark activity there.

I called Miss Troy back. Nothing on the trace, nothing on the caller Parson. I asked if he had asked for me. Miss Troy answered affirmative. "What about Dill? He ask for me too?"

"Yes, sir."

I was puzzled because nobody outside was supposed to know I was working with Dill. I wondered how Parson had the connection. And Dill wouldn't have asked for me by name. His own code name would automatically have funneled it through. We try not to use names. Names can get loose and get you known and help you get yourself punched out or otherwise messed.

I didn't call Burr because you keep away from him unless you need help. We were hired to function. He didn't try to reach me, and we kept things that way the rest of the day while I finished my reports.

When I left, the outer office was without the ineffable presence and light of Miss Troy. It didn't look the same.

I got into my car. It didn't blow up when I fired the starter. I drove out of the lot into the night wondering if Debbie Hill was having dinner in her new apartment alone.

I found that hard to believe.

Five

After nine in L.A. the day people turn in and the whacky night people come on. They're different from the day people, with their own nocturnal rhythms, their own hangups, and they have a lot of the city all to themselves after the tube watchers turn in. There are all-night markets, bars, clubs and swinging spots for singles and swapping. Opportunities for the sexual-minded, regulars and deviates. Leather and gay bars do well, and for the criminal-minded, the town is right there, ready for the taking.

The night people play their own kind of games, and not all of it comes under the heading of fun. Not clean fun, anyway. Maybe the moon has something to do with it. It affects tides, and it can work on people. The crazies come out of the woodwork and play with their own sets of rules.

I ate and nursed a few drinks at a small pub on Pico which featured a good low-keyed musical group, and some awfully pretty young girls serving drinks and showing a lot of flawless skin front and back. The Levi-clad singer holding his mike was bald prematurely, and he had to work a little harder at his love ballads. When the listeners began entwining hands with stars showing in their eyes, I knew I was out of my scene and left.

I tooled around West L.A. and Beverly Hills and swung toward Hollywood down Sunset. The night people were out, women in nightgowns walking their dogs, hippies strumming guitars, kids running drag races between lights. The saloons were getting more crowded and noisier, transvestites hanging outside the gay bars teetering on high platform wedgies, primping, whistling at passing cars. Dogs barked. Women laughed. The little houses off the boulevard put out their lights one by one.

I passed Dante's Dynasty about midnight. It was on a small side street, a block away from one of the better belly joints. The exotic dancers, synthetic and imported, drop the veils and shimmy every glistening inch of their anatomy trying to keep up with loud and terrible music. I decided that if Dante's proved a big nothing, I might take in some of it and watch the girls sweat at their trade. You throw a few bills on the floor to show your appreciation after the first thirty minutes of the gyrating figure with the churning belly, and you get an extra performance of all-out effort, the marvelous navel undulating right under your nose, the near-naked girl enticing you almost out of your shoes.

Dante's was dark and closed, like most hair salons after nightfall. It was set between an art-and-framing shop and a custom-tailor store. Junipers were spaced along the cracking sidewalk, the acid berries they drop ruining the tops and hoods of any car parked beneath their spreading branches.

I drove around the block and didn't see any dark sedans parked with sinister-looking men. There weren't any loading trucks, no nonchalant loungers across the street or at the corner. I wheeled the heap into Dante's driveway. A car was parked behind the small building, lights out, no sign of life. The car looked familiar and I got out to take a better look at it.

It was a beat-up Chevy, gun-metal-gray finish, and it looked like Dill/Bradshaw's, only he wasn't inside it. I walked across the tar-topped driveway to the rear entrance. I tried the door. It wasn't locked and I went in.

I smelled it right away and didn't want to go any farther. He was sitting up in one of the front booths, a hair drier over his head, the exposed copper-wire lead wrapped around his scorched hand. The stench from the burning flesh and hair was overpowering but I still had to know it was my man, Dill.

I pulled out the plug, and when I pushed away the metal hair drier I saw that it was Dill/Bradshaw, all right, looking awfully surprised and shocked at the fact that he was dead. There wasn't anything about his face to suggest any punching around, but the raw red flesh was as good a finish as anyone could ask for, friend or foe.

I called Lieutenant Camino to share my end of the news. I had taken him out of a warm sack plenty of times before, but he never seemed able to get used to it. "Jesus," he said finally, "why the hell can't you stay home at night like other people?"

"I can't help myself, Nick. I've this compulsion to go out and find dead bodies."

"Okay, I'll send somebody over." His tone softened. "Was he a friend?"

I thought about it. "No, I never thought of Dill that way. He was a good operator. Did his job and let you do yours."

"Yeah—well, too bad, anyway. Where you heading next?"

I thought about that, too. "Maybe I'll drop over to ask Dante a few questions."

Camino laughed harshly. "At this hour? He'll kill you."

"He runs a men's beauty shop," I said. "You kidding?"

"Okay, so maybe his wife will kill you. Either way, I'm going back to bed."

"Just one question, Nick—anything new on the Felix Witter murder?"

"Witter? Why you interested in that one?"

"I happened to be there when he went down. I checked with Doc Shipman next day and found out he was poisoned." The scene replayed in my mind's eye. "A nasty way to die."

"*You* should be so lucky," Camino said.

He hung up. I took another look at Dill under the hair drier and wondered what that was all about. I poked around the jars and bottles and jugs along Dante's shelves, and couldn't find anything more incriminating than the fact that a lot of men were using dye for their hair. There certainly was no snowfall. No coke, no heroin, no nothing but Dill on that chair. Maybe he had been talking about dandruff, after all. They say that stuff can kill your chances.

Six

The name slot in the apartment mailbox had him down as Firpo Dante. The apartment number was 211. I went up the concrete steps and walked a narrow deck overlooking a wide concrete courtyard dotted with potted plants. It was an hour after midnight, the whacko night people were out, and I was another in their ranks now, listening outside Firpo Dante's door. I didn't hear anything. All the other apartments were dark and silent, too. Only an occasional light was visible in any of the other apartment buildings in the area. They go to bed early in this town and don't try to fight it.

I rapped softly on Dante's door, heard no response and pressed the bell. I heard soft chimes inside. I waited for the effects to end and jammed the button again. The door suddenly yawned open in front of my face. A man stood in the darkness of the doorway. He wore skimpy trunks, nothing else, and the moonlight revealed a short, chubby angry little man staring up at me with black, glittering eyes. His voice was unsmoothed gravel filtering through a snarl. "The hell you want?"

"Mr. Dante?"

"Yeah. What the hell you want busting in here?"

"Are you the owner of Dante's Dynasty?"

His voice lifted impatiently. "Jesus, yeah—what about it? Is it on fire or something?"

"A man was found murdered a little while ago in your shop."

His hands clenched and unclenched. "Oh yeah? So why come to me about it? Let the police—"

I wagged my head and stopped him. "I'm a private investigator. This man was a friend of mine."

He lifted his hands palms up. "Well, I'm real sorry, Jack. I don't know nothing about it."

I took a step forward, lifting my hand toward the chance of his slamming the door shut. "Well, that's the trouble, Mr. Dante. There's a chance that you might know something about it. I don't want to lean on you but—Mind if I come in and ask a few questions?"

Dante was an impatient man. His right hand shot out while I was still mouthing the last few inane words. He yanked me toward him, and as I stumbled off-balance into his dark living room, he clubbed me behind the neck and I went to my knees. He hit me again and drove my face into his carpeting. Then he kicked me in the ribs with his bare foot and began yelling at me to get up so he could kill me.

Hindsight reminded me how deceptive these roly-poly types can be, the visible blubber hiding the muscles under the skin. You don't have to look like Mr. America to have great natural strength, and I've been surprised before by men without particularly outstanding physiques. Hairdressers aren't necessarily of the gay set, although some are, but plenty of the gay ones have won local and national weight-lifting and body-building titles, too.

I didn't have time to ask Mr. Dante what prizes he had won because I was the big one at the moment, and too punched-out to get up and demand a replay. While my primitive brain was cursing and jumping around, yelling at me to do something, the mainline wires were temporarily disconnected, and I lay there like a felled tree waiting to have my branches trimmed.

A small part of another brain that was still functioning reminded me I was still alive, this was my lucky night, and to stay put and cool. Bells stopped clanging in my head and I heard a small feminine voice sounding petulant and sexy. "Firpo," it said, "where are you? What's going on?"

I remembered Camino telling me that Dante would kill me for disturbing him at such a late hour, and that if he didn't, his wife probably would.

Soft footsteps padded across the carpeting. My eyes rolled up and I saw beautifully formed naked legs. The rest of her was covered by a short Baby Doll nightie starting about halfway between hip and knee. The knees were dimpled, as they always should be, and stopped a few feet away.

"Who is this?" the Baby Doll person said. "What's this big ape doing in here?"

"Don't worry your little head about it, Frannie," Dante said. "Go back to bed. I'll get rid of him and be right with you."

Baby Doll didn't move. Certain women are known to have a blind obstinate streak. Frannie nursed hers along. "But who is he? What's he doing down there? What's going on?"

Dante growled at her, shaking his hand. "Look, will ya cut out? Do me a favor and just go back to bed. I can handle this."

Dante moved his foot to prod me. The last warning bell tolled inside my head. The system remembered suddenly how to do things. Martial sounds flooded my insides and the controller down there asked for a little more adrenalin, please.

I reached out and grabbed Dante's big toe. He lifted his foot and howled. I rolled over, reached up and hit him behind the knee with my other hand. Dante's leg buckled and he went down.

Judo on the ground has three subdivisions: immobilization holds, dislocation locks, neck locks. All three are called *newaza*, meaning groundwork. If you have a pet throw, it's called *tokuiwaza*, and you take it from there. I didn't know exactly what a big-toe grapple was called, but leg entanglement brought him down.

I spun him as he fell, putting him on his back. There were a lot of things I knew how to do from this point on, leg locks, sliding collar locks, applying pressure with my legs over his shoulders, squeezing him until he strangled.

But I remembered Dante ran a hairdressing salon, was roly-poly and overweight, even if he had managed to deck me, and he also had a very cute doll for the evening, which was a lot more fun in store for him than breaking his ribs. So like the jolly good samaritan, instead of doing all those rotten things to him and making him look bad in front of his girl, I slid across the intervening space and sat on his chest.

"Look, I didn't come up here to hurt you," I said. "Only to ask a few questions."

Dante blinked looking up at me and his lips framed a snarl. I showed him my hands, ready to strike, cut and maim, callused, bruised and misshapen by all that damn karate.

"Okay?" I said. "Now take it easy. Relax. Just a few questions and I'll be out of here and you can continue with your evening's entertainment. Okay?"

I felt a shoulder tap and looked up. Baby Doll Frannie was standing over my right shoulder, holding a very large ashtray in her hand. "Look, mister," she said, "I wanna ask *you* a question, too, if you don't mind." Her voice rose several notches. "What the hell you doing up here?"

I knew vaudeville was long dead and attempts to revive it had proved fruitless. Yet somehow I found myself being suckered into an impoverished reversion of yesterday. "If you don't mind, miss—this is strictly between Mr. Dante here and myself. I want to ask him—"

"Well, screw him," she said. "I want to know for myself. What's going on?"

Dante's belly tensed. He could have been laughing inwardly or preparing to clobber me sneakily again if I let myself get distracted. I shook my head stubbornly, hearing huge sighs from the ghosts of the past. "Just hold on, miss. Now, Mr. Dante, let's get back to my original question—"

Something swished and crashed down upon my skull, shattering it into a million splintered pieces. I wanted to tell her this was no way to conduct an interrogation, but the rockets going off inside my head signaled me to knock it off. Ashtrays can be lethal when properly applied. This one was, and I tumbled off my perch on Dante's ribs and fell headlong through his carpet.

The cool night air braced me. The moon was spectacular, prismatic, each section floating between fragmented patches of clouds. My hands felt cold stone. I looked up. My head cleared and I saw the closed door with the numbers on it. 211 it said, and I was back where I had started, outside Dante's apartment.

I couldn't think of the Japanese phrase for sitting on his chest, and offhand settled for *stupido*. Camino's words came back to mock me, and I listened closely this time. I wanted to get up and go in again, but Camino was telling me over again that either Dante or his wife would kill me for disturbing them at this hour. Camino, being connected with Homicide, ought to know.

I got up and found I could walk funny. Then I went down the steps and into my car and went home. The town was wide open, all the whacko night people out having fun, playing games, bashing heads in, making asses of themselves. This time I felt a certain kinship with them. Tonight they were all my brothers, all the whacky ones out there, and I wished them well.

Seven

Camino made the wheel go full circle by waking *me* up the next morning. In my line of work, getting hit over the head at times is normal procedure. But detaching the head from the pillow was a lesson in stoicism. Perhaps there had been too many bonks on the noggin already and the little workers inside were getting tired of the mending work, goofing off instead of staying on the assembly line, and letting me shift for myself with an ersatz head.

I said hello softly so as not to disturb any work in progress. Camino was apparently well with an unzonked skull and could afford to talk loudly.

"We found a body in the chair, like you said. Any idea why he was knocked off?"

"I got a message he was covering some big drug deal at Dante's."

"Find anything?"

"Only Dill. Body in a chair."

"Yeah," Camino said, "about that . . . They don't knock off too many guys in your racket that way, I hope—do they?"

"Somebody made it a first. I hope to find him someday."

"Frankly, I hope you do too. Okay." I could see him at his desk crossing out the questions on the pad. "Now, you said something about going over to query the owner of the shop— Mr. Dante."

"Yeah, I did that. This time it happens you were right."

"About what?"

"You said Dante would try to kill me for disturbing him late at night, and if he didn't, his wife would."

"Oh? We got Dante down here. Says he's not married."

"Well, some cute little dingaling he had there can make it to the finals if they allow a hitting-with-ashtray event in the next Olympics."

Camino laughed. My head stopped mending with all that noise. "Oh, that was Miss Corbett. Francine Corbett. Dante's girl friend." He laughed some more. "What happened to all that karate you're supposed to be such a whiz at?"

I shook my head and was reminded not to do that ever again. "The hairdresser decked me when I went in and Gentleman Jim's daughter skulled me when I was getting better, and finished me off. I think karate is only good on little girls when they're tying their shoelaces."

"Okay," Camino said after he finished a few more guffaws. "I just wanted your side of it to know how to answer their complaint about your invading the privacy of his home and all that."

"Whatever they say, as long as I don't have to pay for breaking their favorite ashtray with my head."

"I'll let you straighten that out with him later when he gets back to his shop. Dante's got six hair stylists working for him, including Miss Corbett, whom you've already met. I've got their names and addresses in the event you want to keep on making a horse's ass of yourself about this thing."

I forgot about my wounded head and exploded. "Listen, Lieutenant, one of our guys was killed. I went to Dante's on a tip from his last message."

"Think you can remember it?"

I did and Camino was silent a few seconds. "Dante's Dynasty Sunset Snowfall? That it?"

"Right, Nick. What the hell else could he have meant other than a big drop of cocaine?"

"I don't know. What time did he give you his message?"

"About three o'clock. I didn't get it personally. He phoned it in to Miss Troy. She said she could have sworn it was Dill speaking."

"What the hell's so unusual about that?"

"Some other joker had just called to tell me to write Dill off, that he'd been had, punched out and taken to a green car."

"Did he give you anything on the make and model?"

"He was about to, but I think they shot him."

"Jesus," Camino said. "Who was this guy?"

"Some creep. Parson. Works the undercover bit."

"Ex–vice squad," Camino said, growling to himself. "I always figured Parson to be more of a bastard than a creep. Unless— maybe we're both right. Now, anytime you wanna kill *that* sonofabitch, it's all right with me."

"*Muchas gracias, compadre,* but as I said, I think Parson already bought it. Sounded like a big gun wearing a silencer."

"Too bad." Camino sounded disappointed. "I think I always wanted you to kill him as a personal favor to me. He stepped all over a lot of people, that bastard Parson."

"Okay," I said. "If he's gone, tell me somebody else you don't like, maybe I can run down and knock a head off before breakfast."

"It'll take a while. I don't want to waste one." Camino was sounding gloomy again. "Listen, what time did you get to Dante's?"

"About midnight. Walked in, found Dill and called you. What was it, about twelve-fifteen then?"

Camino sighed. "Well, yeah, something like that, I guess."

"Okay, what's bothering you?"

"Oh, it ain't much. Our medical examiner was down there before one. His report said your man Dill hadn't been dead quite an hour."

"Jesus," I said, "you're telling me he could have been knocked off just a few moments before I got there?"

"Yeah," Camino said. "Something like that. Or a few minutes after you got there."

I wasn't sure if he was laughing when he hung up.

I burned the bacon and the toast, the egg yolks got messed, and I was out of coffee, or nearly. Only three small teaspoons left in the can and I needed at least six. It seemed like the start for one hell of a good day.

I went through the morning paper and checked two possible winners. Before I could make a call and put my money down, the doorbell told me to throw on a robe and answer the door.

She was blond, beautiful, maybe pressing thirty-five, slim but curved in all the right places, very snazzily dressed, the kind that don't waste their time calling on me often.

"My name is Marilyn Channing. You're Mr. Roper?"

There weren't any back-up thugs behind her with wrenches or blow darts. I showed her the living-room sofa, the chair, the newspapers tossed on the floor. She stopped halfway past the kitchen, sniffing. "Something is burning."

"Something *was* burning. What can I do for you, Miss Channing?"

"*Mrs.* Channing—that is, I was." She looked at the sofa and chair, made a quick judgment call and picked the chair. She crossed a leg over her knee better than I had ever seen it done. I had to give the legs 10 out of a possible 10, also. "A friend gave me your name. I understand you're some kind of detective."

I wanted my chair back, but she was in it and didn't look the least bit anxious for arm perchers. "What's the name of the friend, Mrs. Channing?" I had my gun somewhere but needed a better reason for shooting her than her taking my favorite armchair. But she was opening her handbag, and her secret weapon looked more like a checkbook.

"Debbie Hill. You see, we both knew Felix Witter rather well."

I made for the bottle stand. "I wouldn't want you telling Miss Hill I make rotten coffee. How about a drink?"

I had her pegged, and she knew it and nodded. "Vodka straight up."

I handed her her drink and poured one for myself, pulled over a hard chair and sat down, primly drawing my old robe tight so as not to excite her.

44

Her eyes were a brilliant green, the kind that could gleam if they had to. "I came to see you," she said, "because I'm interested in finding out who killed Felix."

"Right now, so are the police, Mrs. Channing. What makes you think I can do a better job than the regular forces?"

"You'll have better motivation," she said. She put her checkbook down on her silken knee and pressed it flat. "Name your price."

She wasn't into more than half a vodka jigger so far, so it had to be something else. "The price varies," I said. "You can do better by telling me more about you and Felix Witter."

She looked cross. "I was in love with the sonofabitch. And for him I left my husband Frank, whom I loved dearly. I loaned Felix lots of money for his business enterprises. He died still owing me."

I nodded sympathetically. "What do we call lots of money in your league?"

"Try two hundred thousand. Plus a bit more at some of the better men's shops. Felix did like good clothes."

I padded back for a refill. She declined one with a shake of her glossy head. "So we're talking about like a quarter-million you doodled on Mr. Witter?"

She raised her glass. "That's close enough. And that's why I want you to catch up with the sonofabitch who killed him. Frankly, if Felix had lived, I'm pretty sure he still would have stiffed me for the money. But he was such a gorgeous hunk of man, and it was such fun pretending to myself that I'd get it all back someday."

I shrugged. "But he is dead, Mrs. Channing. And even supposing I do catch whoever did the job on him, that still won't help you get your money back."

She tilted the glass and drained it. Her lips looked wet and luscious. I could have had fun with her without the two hundred fifty thousand.

"I know it won't," she said somewhat harshly. "But after what I put out, I don't like somebody else cutting in and spoiling all my fun. Know what I mean?"

"You want revenge."

She slapped her checkbook. "You're damn right. Now tell me how much and I'll get out of here, and you can go back to your handicapping."

I pushed the paper away with my foot. "Nothing special going today, and I don't feel that lucky." I looked her over and she didn't mind. "Now, *you* look like something special. Mind telling me how something like Witter could have scrambled your brains so?"

She stood up, pale, erect and trembling. She was all sex and I could have had her merely by reaching out for her. Again she sensed my reading.

"Well, hell, that's what it's supposed to be all about, anyway, isn't it? Somebody like that a woman just has to have in the sack. He looked so much, you couldn't help but think he was going to give you more than anything, more than anybody."

I indicated the pad on the table. "You can put down your number. I'll call you if I come up with anything."

She tossed her head, the green eyes flashing. I sat on the chair and she waited another bit, then grabbed the pen and dashed off something in a fast scribble.

"There's also another thing," I said.

"Yes?" Her pose was just naturally graceful. I was getting to hate Felix Witter with surprising intensity.

"If you're a friend of Debbie Hill, you may know I put the same question to her. It goes for everybody. How would I know you didn't kill Witter yourself?"

She didn't look surprised or offended. She just gave me the gleaming eyes. They spelled out *s-c-r-e-w y-o-u J-a-c-k!* Then she turned her back to me and walked toward the door. All my millions of hungry, thwarted animal cells wanted her, but I let them go hungry, punishing the little bastards.

I was still sitting there when she got the door open. She nodded coolly and pulled it shut behind her. I knew I didn't have Mrs. Channing fooled for a moment either. She knew damn well I was afraid to get up and walk her to the door.

Eight

His picture was stamped on a small yellow placard in a Santa Monica store window. He was posed in the right-side biceps and shoulder with the side of the leg flexed. The small type under it read: *Felix Witter—Mr. Europe, Mr. World, Mr. Olympia, Mr. Universe—uses Explosive INSTA-POWER, the High-Protein drink to BULK UP. Gain 10 pounds in 10 days. Powder dissolves easily in milk. Tastes like milk shake.*

The big sign over the store said GOOD EARTH THINGS.

People had to pass a reading test to get inside to the store shelves. NO BARE FEET. NO DOGS ALLOWED. NO CHECKS CASHED.

The young fellow behind the counter was happy to see somebody up that early shopping for nutrients. He sported a lot of hair, a straggly beard and a pale, pasty complexion. He was thin, slight-shouldered, narrow-chested, his lips bloodless.

"Good morning," he said softly. "Can I help you, sir?"

I halted, veering off to check the signs and display racks. REJUVENATE WITH GENUINE SIBERIAN GINSENG! *Yam flakes. Toasted soy beans. Karob. Yeast flakes. Biochemic salts.* LYSINE. THREONINE. ASPARTIC ACID AND ASPARAGUS. GARLIC AND PARSLEY. COBALAMIN—B 12. PYRIDOXIN—B 6. PANTO-THENATE—B 3.

The paperback books in the revolving rack had a general appeal. *Are You Radioactive? Common Sense and Arthritis.*

47

Natural Childbirth. There's Hope for Cancer. Secrets of Aging Successfully. Little Known Facts About Your Gonads. Zinc and Its Part in Your Health. You Need Not Be Bald.

There were signs for vegetarian facial and tanning creams. Organically grown carrots, dates and figs. Comfrey tea for bowel stasis. Cider vinegar—the miracle drink. Avocado soap with lecithin.

The clerk was still glad to see me when I came over, apparently unfazed about looking weak and anemic while surrounded by the glut of organic and nutritional food goodies.

I depressed my chest cage and waved my hand weakly. "My doctor suggested I ought to try some vitamins. Not enough energy lately. Trouble sleeping. Dizzy spells. No appetite. That sort of thing."

The clerk frowned. "Well, of course, that could all be psychosomatic, you know. I mean, I can sell you a lot of stuff, but have you looked at yourself lately?"

"Just this morning—shaving."

He shook his head reprovingly. "Oh no, I mean inside. Your personal psyche can give you a blueprint of yourself if you could relax and let your defenses down. Higher and older forces at work, you see. Your dreams, too. They can tell you a lot about yourself. About what's happening to you. Do you remember any dreams?"

"Well, no," I said. "With the trouble I have sleeping, I guess I don't dream too much."

"Oh yes, you do." He bobbed his head, his Adam's apple escalating. "Everybody dreams. But far too few pay attention to what their dreams are telling them."

"I think my last dream told me to come down here and stock up on some vitamins."

"Oh?" He frowned and looked me over carefully. "Well, like I said, I can always sell you vitamins. But they're not the complete answer, despite what your doctor said. Vitamins can only do so much for you, you see. The main thing is to rejuvenate yourself through a more spiritual diet."

I nodded. "That makes sense."

48

"Now, you look to me like a meat eater. Is that true?"

"Yes. A lotta meat. Steak, roast beef, chops—all that stuff."

He threw his pale thin hands apart dramatically. "Well, there you are, you see? The human body wasn't meant to be a garbage dump. There are no vibrations to meat because it's a dead product, you see? But plants—vegetables actually have auras, you know. Some people can actually see them, just as they can on humans. If you want to revitalize yourself, you really should start with energizing your cells through proper diet, and that means, of course, with growing things. No meat. Meat does absolutely nothing for a person but give him the illusion he is being well-nourished. Whereas fasting and a strict vegetable and fruit diet, with some seed products, will give you all the energy and strength you need."

"Is that how you do it?"

He nodded emphatically. "Oh yes. I've been on it for years now. The body doesn't need fat and decomposed flesh which is all you get from your meat diet. All it will get you in the end is high blood pressure and possibly a heart attack."

"What about eggs? You eat eggs?"

"Oh Lord, no! Eggs are protein, yes—but loaded with cholesterol, you see. Bad for the heart." He tapped his denim shirt over the heart area. "You can get all the protein you need from leaf vegetables and your legumes."

"How about milk? I heard that—"

He shook his head. "How can milk be any good for you when a cow has seven stomachs? You can't expect your one stomach to process what *it* produces, can you?"

Just thinking about it was giving me heartburn. "All right," I said. "I'll give it a try. Now, what can you give me in the vitamin and mineral department?"

He frowned. "Well, you know, there are additional supplements to the original supplements." He started to tick them off on his fingers. "There's rutin, and niacinamide. Lecithin, lycines, enzymes, folic acid, pantothenate, glutamine, lipoic acid—"

"Fine," I said. "I'll take 'em."

He looked at me surprised. "All?"

I nodded, firmly rubbing the heartburn away. "And while you're at it, there's a product Felix Witter endorses—you know, the Mr. America–Mr. Universe fellow—I'd like that, too."

My salesclerk sniffed. "Well, if you really want it—but it's really nothing, won't do a thing for you."

"But I understand it's a high-protein—a very big seller in these stores."

He shook his head again. "Very good for Mr. Witter, then, but actually, if you'll listen to me, it's nothing but sugar, milk and cellulose—and you can get more high protein in one little peanut than you can in a whole big bottle of Mr. Witter's High-Protein wafers. That goes for his Insta-Power drink, too."

I smiled winningly. "I know you're right, but I'd like to try it, anyway. If you knew what he looked like, you'd understand the appeal of his—"

I was cut off. "Oh, I know what he looked like. I've seen his pictures. All those useless pounds of muscle doing absolutely nothing for him but give his heart an extra burden to carry around. I can assure you, Felix Witter didn't get that development by eating his product."

I bit my lip convincingly, I hoped, as otherwise this act wasn't worth bleeding for. "He didn't?"

"Certainly not. He was a weight lifter. One of those dumb iron freaks. At it all day, lifting I don't know how many tons a day— But, look, if you want to buy it, it's your money, after all—"

I shot my best smile. "Well, just a small bottle or two. If it doesn't work, I'll tell all my friends."

"W-e-l-l . . ."

I followed him around the shelves and helped him carry the big bag back to the counter. He added it all up on the tape and it came to a nice profit for whoever was running this chain of stores. I put down the bills, got very little change, and he thanked me a lot. As I was leaving, he told me to remember to take lots of the B vitamins he had given me.

"Is that to counter the booze?" I said.

His pale eyes were surprised. "Oh no. It won't hurt, of course, but you're not supposed to take any alcohol at all in your system. Alcohol interferes with your oxygen consumption, you see, paralyzes the hormones there, and you can't breathe properly."

"Are you sure?" I said, anxious to get away from this sincere and well-meaning spoilsport.

"Oh yes. Also look at all those tiny blood vessels over your nose and cheeks next time you have a chance. You don't think that's any sign of health, do you?"

I took the freshly lit cigarette off my lip. "I suppose you don't think too much of cigarette smoking, either."

"On the contrary," he said. "I recommend the steady inhalation of nicotine and its by-products, especially if a person wishes to shorten his life span by six minutes for each cigarette he smokes."

It was all as depressing as I figured this morning was going to be.

Nine

I dropped the health-food junk on a table and called Debbie Hill. I was hoping she would be pleased that I was helping to move her health items off the shelf, and invite me over to her pad to talk about this and that.

She wasn't any faster answering her phone than her doorbell. "I'm in a hurry. Who's this?"

"Max Roper. You may remember—"

"Oh yes, of course. I was just leaving. Is this anything important?"

"I'm not sure. A Mrs. Marilyn Channing was in to see me this morning. Said she was a friend of yours, and you gave her my name. True or false?"

"Well, yes, I know Marilyn . . ."

"She wants to hire me to find whoever killed Felix Witter. Did she tell you that?"

"We didn't go into it, if that's what you mean. Now if—"

It was more fun interrupting than I had thought. I was getting to understand why people do it. "That's kind of odd, isn't it? Two women in love with the same man—being friends."

She was crisp, still sounding in a hurry. Pushing health foods can apparently energize a person, too. "We're not that close, exactly. But I've known Marilyn and her husband Frank for years. She wanted a name, somebody who could do a job, I gave her yours. She's got enough money to make it worth your while."

"That's what she tried to tell me. I'm curious about who was last in Mr. Witter's life. You or Mrs. Channing?"

"I'm sorry, but I really don't have time to go into that now. If you'll—"

"Can you spare a little time tonight? I'd like to talk some more about this."

"I'll be back about seven. Give me a call then and we'll see."

"Just one more question, Miss Hill, and I'll let you fly. Who puts out the Felix Witter products?"

"That would be Healthfare Organics. The HO line."

"Fine. Who's the man behind the checking account?"

"That would be Mr. Johnny Albany. I'm sorry, but that's all I can—"

"Okay. Thanks for your time. I'll call you—"

She was probably out the door already, making those beautiful legs earn their keep. I got up to put the health-food stuff away. I wondered if the Felix Witter product could do anything for that lump on my head. I tried the bottle with his miracle High-Protein wafer first. It tasted a little sweet but not bad. The bump felt the same. I needed milk for the Insta-Power drink. I don't keep milk. I mixed some of the powder with a little booze and water. It wasn't too bad.

The doorbell buzzed. I went to get it, still screwing the cap on the bottle. I saw the mailman through the peephole and opened the door. Somebody moved fast from the side and put a gun on my nose. He was bigger than I was and the gun felt like a Smith & Wesson .38, which made him a lot bigger. The mailman was knocked aside and I saw the other guy there with a chopped-down shotgun leveled at my fly. The mailman tried to tell me with frightened eyes that he wasn't a willing partner to this dastardly scheme, and I accepted his apology as silently because there were more important things to worry about.

I didn't know either of the two big apes, but they didn't need calling cards with what they carried. The shotgun prodded my ribs.

"You're Roper, right? Let's move it."

The other man on my right lifted the gun off my nose and tapped the bridge two times. The gun metal didn't flake off and I could tell it was a good gun. His arm retracted a few inches now and he held the Smith & Wesson off my right ear. Any loud noise from that near point would have severely damaged my hearing, although fortunately I wouldn't have been alive long enough then to worry about needing a hearing aid.

"Downstairs," the man said. "No funny stuff."

I tried but couldn't think of anything funny enough. There are a lot of good moves one can make with karate, but they're a lot tougher to do with a gun stuck in one ear and a shotgun inches away from blasting out your necessary body parts and vital fluids.

I managed to shake my head in a rueful way. "You got to be kidding about the funny stuff. Can't you jokers see what I'm holding?"

The shotgun moved back a few inches. "What's he holding, Charley?"

Smith-Wesson sounded cross. "How the hell I know? Looks like a jar something."

I held Felix Witter's bottle of Insta-Power up a fraction, label toward me. "Right, Charley," I said. "Only you got to know what's in the jar that makes it so funny."

Smith-Wesson scowled. "Okay, so what's in it?"

"Explosive. That's what's in it. I can drop it and make us all blow up, or you can shoot me and we all go up. Which way do you want it?"

Shotgun took a step back and wiped his mouth, holding his piece with the other hand, pretty much as it was. "He's off his nut. Take it away from him, Charley."

I turned myself and the bottle more toward him. "No, you take it. Maybe I can drop it between us and get you and me for sure, and Charley for a possible hit."

He sniffed, scowled and shifted a half-step away. "You crazy, you goddamn nut? Why you wanna do that? Blow yourself up, too—for what?"

Charley spoke. "Shuddup, Lew. Why we arguing with this jerk? What kinda explosive, Roper, and how come you got it?"

"You know me and my work, guys. This stuff has been tested and I was about to deliver it downtown to the FBI office when you called."

Charley didn't like anybody mentioning the FBI. "Yeah? What's it called?"

I remembered my health-food store training. "Threonine." I took a chance that neither was up to reading and turned the jar so they could see part of the label. "See for yourself—it's marked Explosive Insta-Power! If you boys were in the army, you'd know all about threonine. If you weren't, you just picked a bad day to call."

Charley had his gun lowered now. He looked at Lew. "I never hearda no three-oh-nine. You?"

Lew shrugged. "I think maybe—I ain't sure."

"So whattaya think?"

"Unless it's all bull . . . I dunno."

"You think it's bull—ask the mailman. He knows I don't kid around. Ask him what happened the last time."

They turned to the mailman. He looked pale and frightened enough to convince anybody of horrible things he had witnessed.

"What about it, you?" Charley said.

The mailman gulped and swallowed nervously. "You better take his word for it, fellers. The man knows his business."

Charley turned back to me, scowling but not as tough. "Okay, so tell us. The same stuff?"

I nodded smugly. "Pretty much. That batch was lysine—not quite as potent. But you can still see the damage on the walls and ceiling. The other two guys they scraped off."

Charley squinted wisely. "So how come you're in one piece?"

I thanked the gods of lousy building inspection and maintenance, and jerked my head back to the door open behind me. "I managed to get back inside and shut the door while it was still in the air on its way down."

Charley looked at Lew. "I think we oughtta forget it, huh? Whattaya think?"

Lew shrugged. He pulled his piece up to his side. "Whatever you say, Charley. You ask me, it ain't worth it. The guy looks crazy enough to do it one more time."

Charley nodded and put his gun back under his arm inside the holster. "Yeah, the hell with it. They ask us what happened, the creep wasn't home."

"That's good thinking," I said. "Try me again. Chances are, next time I won't have any of this stuff around and you'll have me cold."

Lew nodded. "Sure. It makes sense."

Charley backed off another step. "Okay, so we'll forget this one. Okay?"

I smiled pleasantly, shaking the powder in the jar. "Mind telling me what this was all about? Who sent you boys?"

Charley managed a fierce grin. "Hey, don't press your luck, you know what I mean?"

I shrugged, apparently disappointed. "Okay. Then maybe you can do me a small favor." They both eyed me carefully. "I had a little battery trouble with the car and couldn't get it started. Maybe you can give me a lift downtown to the Feds office so I can drop this stuff off."

They looked at me as if I had suddenly sprouted a contagious cancer, circled the mailman and backed off. Then in unison, they bolted and ran down the steps.

The mailman exhaled vigorously and mopped his brow. "Jesus, that was close. You get that kinda visitors often?"

"Not since the last time, remember?" I flipped my spare hand and closed the door behind me. A timid knock sounded almost instantly and I opened it again.

He was holding out a small manila envelope. "Sorry, I forgot. Ten cents postage due on this one."

I gave it to him for the overweight circular and went back inside. I headed straight for the kitchen and took the cap off the jar and poured myself a lot of the powder and topped it with a good belt of my favorite dissolving liquid.

Then I raised my glass and drank a silent grateful toast to the memory of Felix Witter.

Ten

Johnny Albany was the living answer to a jock's dream—a former weight man and body builder who had pumped his hundred-odd tons of iron a day for enough years to win himself the Mr. America title. That was ten years back, and in the meantime Johnny Albany had parlayed his loving cups and publicity into a million-dollar-a-year business manufacturing and pushing vitamin-supplement products.

Healthfare Organics was only one of the many new health-food companies shooting for the moon, but Albany had been in the racket long enough to have established a firm footing, and because of his background had been able to attract the new champion iron men to his promotion stable. Felix Witter had been the biggest attraction, after himself, and I was curious about how much of a bite Witter was taking out of his boss's take-home pay. It had to be considerable because with his reputation he could have demanded a lot of front money from any outfit. Yet my early-morning visitor, Marilyn Channing, had mentioned the two hundred big ones she had invested in Witter's enterprises, and I had to assume he had put in with Johnny Albany and bought himself a good piece of the Healthfare company.

I had gone through some of the old health and strength mags and found this statistical line on Johnny Albany in his prime:

1965 AAU Mr. America
28 years old
5'10" tall
230 pounds
52" chest
20" arms
27" waist
26" thighs
19" calves

El Segundo always smelled like rotten eggs due to the heavy refinery processing the beach town allowed for its necessary tax dollars. You rolled up your windows and put on the air conditioner until you were past, and then the ocean breeze coming off Manhattan and Hermosa Beaches unsmogged your nasal passages. There were always pretty airline hostesses sunning at the beaches, and they could do a lot toward clearing one's head too.

The factory and showroom was between El Segundo and Manhattan Beach, off Sepulveda, a short ride from my pad in Santa Monica. A long low series of whitewashed boxlike cement-block buildings without any frills. The warehouse was big enough to house a 747 and with commendable foresight and business acumen was backed up to a railroad spur connecting with Southern Pacific lines.

The office showroom had all the products along glass shelves. Johnny Albany's Natural-Organic Vitamin C Liquid. Johnny Albany's Natural-Organic Energex with specially added vitamins and minerals. Johnny Albany's Muscle Rub. Johnny Albany's High-Protein enriched with Bromelain, Papaya and Yeast. Johnny Albany's Yoga-Tone to fight iron deficiency.

On another shelf were others. Mr. America Quik-Energy. Felix Witter's Insta-Power drink. Felix Witter's High-Protein with B 12. Felix Witter's Natural Organic Weight-Plus Power Gainer. Mr. Universe's Natural Organic Protozyme with all the essential amino acids. Felix Witter's Wildman Powerizer.

The Felix Witter line was small but coming along. The jars looked the same, all processed by the same company, Healthfare Organics, headed by Mr. Johnny Albany.

A young lady at the desk looked me over carefully to try to determine if I was buying or selling. To save her time, I asked for Albany.

"What's it about?" she said.

I shrugged. "Business. Also personal."

She tapped her pencil. "Well, which?"

"Tell him Max Roper. Health-food investigator."

She picked up her phone and whispered that somebody from the Board of Health was outside to see him. She listened, nodding several times. "Mr. Albany will be glad to see you. Third door to your left when you go through those double doors."

When I passed her desk, she was busy brushing dust and imaginary specks off its glass-top surface.

He rose from behind his desk to greet me, tanned and unwrinkled, eyes sparkling, teeth whiter than Monday's wash, a big dimple in his chin, slightly Roman-curved nose, looking no worse after ten years away from it than last year's winner. His grip wasn't better than a pair of pliers, and his voice was the hearty purr of the experienced con man.

"Now, what's all this about a Board of Health inspection of our product?"

I shook my head. "Your girl got it wrong. I said I was investigating health foods."

He lifted his outsize shoulders, puzzled. "So what's the difference?"

I gave him my card and showed him the private-eye buzzer, and he read it all through. "I'm trying to find out who didn't like Felix Witter bad enough to kill him."

He still looked puzzled. "Okay. That's one. What's that got to do with the health foods?"

My shoulders weren't as big, but I showed him I knew the shrug too. "You're carrying his line. I understand it's selling well. I had the notion he was getting too big for somebody in the health-food business with a similar line that Witter was hurting."

He had it all now and nodded, pursing his lips. "Well, I don't know. I don't know that his line was selling that much better than mine, and my stuff is out a long time. Anyway, why would I want to kill the bastard? He worked for me, more or less."

"I was thinking more in terms of competitors in the field," I said. "For example, I notice the Good Earth Things store carries Witter's stuff in addition to their own."

Albany grinned. "Well, yeah—that ain't so unusual, actually. I mean, it's done, some . . . but we had, kind of like an 'in' there, you see. What the hell—it's all a big sell, and Felix had a way with the right people."

"Like Debbie Hill?"

He lost his grin and his dark eyes quickly computed my height, weight and muscle tone. "Well, yeah, Debbie was one—she buys and we sell, see? How'd you happen to know about her?"

"Ordinary murder investigation. She was one of Witter's girl friends."

He found out how to grin again. "Listen, pal, you'll be an old man before you check them all out. Know what I mean? They flocked to Felix like—like flames to a moth."

"Then there's a Mrs. Channing who was a friend of his, too, and—"

His eyes lit up. "Marilyn? Oh yeah—now, there's a nice lady for you. But I think you're up the wrong tree if you're pegging her for it. No, man, Marilyn really had the hots for my tiger." He shook his dark curly head. "No, sir. No way she was going to give up any of her action with Felix."

"I understand she had a bit of money out to him—for business purposes. Did Witter buy in with you—was he a partner?"

"Partner?" Albany said. "You got to be kidding, Mac. Business is good. Why would I need a partner?"

I remembered a fragment of what Debbie Hill had told me. Slow delivery on Witter's product. Foul-ups on the assembly line, handling, shipping, or whatever. "Expansion could be a pretty fair reason," I said. "You take in somebody with a little money, and you grow a little bigger. Done all the time by a lot of outfits."

Albany shook his head, maintaining his smug grin. "Not me, pal. You take in a partner, you got to cut him in, right? No, man—I didn't need Witter's money. What I used him for was promotion—his stud quality, you know? The way he looked, half the women in the world wanted to hop into the sack with him.

"Only for me, it was worth just so much. So Witter got a cut, is all. A percentage we worked out according to how he boosted the line. Dig?"

"Sure," I said. "But according to what I heard from my client, Witter had a lot of money to invest. If you didn't get it, where did it go? Or was he running a spin-off—a little health business of his own?"

Albany took a deep breath and showed me what a 52-inch chest could balloon to with some air inside it. "Beats the hell out of me, pal. Maybe he was throwing it away on some of those broads. He traveled a lot, you know. Maybe he fixed up his new pad down at the beach and that took a lot of the bread. I dunno. Far as his own business, forget it. Witter didn't have brains enough to come in outta the rain. He was the type-a guy could run a half-mill into a shoestring."

When he finished laughing at his joke, he glanced at his thin gold watch. He studied it, figured out the time and came back to me. "You don't have to take my word for it, pal. You're a dick, so you know ways to trace anybody who's got a business going. There's all kinds of records downtown, right?"

"All right. So Witter wasn't into your business and had nothing going on his own. I appreciate your taking the time to fill me in. Maybe you can give me some inside dope on the other matter."

Albany frowned. "Which one was that, pal?"

"His murder. I'll have to talk to a lot of the iron men who didn't like him. Maybe you can put me onto somebody who was close to him, knew his moves and so on."

Albany leaned forward on his desk, his hands up tentlike in the Hindu prayer-peace position, and leaned his rugged face against his stiffly held fingers. "You mean you want me to finger some guy for you, huh?"

"Maybe he was a kind of friend of yours, and you didn't like him getting knocked off that way. Maybe it will cost you a few bucks replacing him with another champion. That way, it wouldn't be fingering somebody so much as helping to clear up a murder. The fuzz will be down to talk to you soon enough anyway. If I got a lead, maybe I could beat their time. I'm in business for myself, too, you know."

Albany nodded, his eyes still on mine. "Well, you know, I had reasons to kill the bastard myself. He cut my time with a lotta broads."

I waved my hand, smiling. "Okay, so you might have lost a couple here and there. You look like you do all right."

"Yeah—well, sure—I get something part of the time. It ain't like I'm ready for the wheelchair." He scowled and rubbed the slightly formed jowl under his jaw.

"Just any name," I said quickly, "and I'll be out of here and let you go back to work. Anybody at all who comes to mind who knew Witter and his life style."

He rubbed his hands while I watched the ropelike forearm muscles under his short-sleeved shirt knot and ripple. "There's a couple I can give you. There's Kay Morrow, for instance."

"Kay Morrow. What does she do?"

"I dunno. I think maybe she's hooked up with some smart money now. But what she used—she used to be Witter's wife."

"Living here in town?"

"Yeah, I guess. Here or Vegas. I kinda lost track of Kay." He shook his head wistfully. "Too bad. That kid was really stacked, you know?"

I got up, stuck out my hand. "Well then, I'll be—"

"There's also Shelby," he said moodily.

"Shelby. Who's he?"

"He's Debbie Hill's boss. I think he's got some kinda crush on

Deb, and he also hated Felix's guts for cutting him out. Know what I mean?"

I nodded. "I know what you mean."

He stood up to stretch, taking up most of the available space at his end of the small office. "'I suppose you're wondering why I ain't madder, huh? I mean, after all the guy worked for me, and we know each other a long time pushing the iron. Maybe you don't know, I was Mr. America myself back in sixty-five."

"I know," I said soothingly.

"Well, maybe you don't know I helped Felix get himself together. You know, like I gave him my own exercise and weight routine, how to bring himself along like, all that. Gave him a lotta my time and advice."

I waited.

Albany shrugged, sat on the edge of his desk. "Well, what the hell. He was big. He had the frame. Anybody could see he could make it all the way with the right kind of workouts. Maybe I saw it first, I dunno. But anyway, I put out for the bastard. And you wanna know what?"

I was ready with my cue. "What?"

"The bastard never thanked me. Eight, nine world titles he got and the sonofabitch never said thanks once."

"Maybe it slipped his mind," I offered.

"Nah. The guy was a—what's the word—a egomaniac. Took it all for granted. Like it was coming to him. That was his way, anyhow. I'll take mine, screw everybody else."

I thought there was a glimmer of another clue. "Did he try it with you? Apart from those broads you mentioned."

Albany laughed. He punched his big hamlike fists together. "He wasn't crazy. He was bigger, sure, but I think down deep he knew I could take him any time."

I nodded encouragingly. "He had about thirty pounds on you and a lot of reach. It could have been a good match."

"Yeah," Albany said. "I think so, too. But I coulda taken him. You wanna know why? I'll give you one good reason—the guy was yellow."

I shrugged. "That happens, too. Maybe that was why he

worked so hard to put all that bulk on. To give him a little more confidence."

"It wouldn't matter," Albany said. "You ain't got the heart, it don't matter how much you put on. He knew that, too."

There was another lag and I wondered if the point had come and gone.

"So all in all, what I'm saying is, sure it's too bad the guy had to go out that way, but you look around, you'll be surprised. You won't find anybody crying the sonofabitch is gone."

"Maybe his mother was fond of him," I said.

"Well, if she was, she was the only one. Matter of fact, now that we're talking about it, I'm only surprised somebody didn't knock him off sooner."

"But you didn't," I said.

Albany grinned, his eyes clearly mocking. "Well, no," he said. "Not that way, I wouldn't. The way he got it, that way, whoever did it looked like he was afraid of Felix. Know what I mean?"

I said I did. Albany nodded moodily.

"Yeah, I coulda taken him. Only now the sonofabitch won't never know."

Eleven

He didn't look at all related to his product—Good Earth Things. Titus Shelby was what it said on his door. He wasn't a muscle freak like Johnny Albany, and apart from the class and wealth he exuded, seemed normal. He was a tall man in his mid-forties, hair graying at the sides, handsome in a patrician way, cold-eyed. He didn't try to break my fingers off with a hearty handshake. He didn't see my hand out there.

"What can I do for you, Mr. Roper? My secretary said you're an investigator."

"It's about the murder of Felix Witter. I know you've been in the health-food business for a long time. Your Good Earth Things stores carry his line put out by another company. That's one of the things I'd like to ask you about."

Shelby had one expression and didn't let any passing or tangential thoughts tamper with it. "Not unusual. We produce a certain number of health foods for our chain of stores. We purchase some of good quality from other companies. We make more on our own product, naturally. Regarding Felix Witter's line, it sold rather well due to his reputation in the body-building sport. Better than Johnny Albany's own similar product, which we tried for a while formerly. Witter's line is dead now, of course, and we may go with the new champion."

Checking the aftermath had slipped my mind. "The new Mr. Universe? Who took it?"

"Mr. Eddie Blue."

Quickly balancing my forgetful side, I remembered Eddie Blue hotfooting it up Debbie Hill's walk the morning after the event. Eddie already had a double win in the Mr. Universe contest, I recalled, and the new triumph put him at a par with Felix Witter in that big and very important international event.

"Yes," Titus Shelby said, adding mind reading to his act of being too good for the rest of the world, "Blue now has a triple Mr. Universe, equaling Felix Witter's record. So I would imagine he might prove a safe investment for us."

"Does that mean you intend putting out the new Eddie Blue line yourself, or are you in competition with other companies for his name?"

"It depends," Shelby said, agreeable to letting it go at that.

I wrinkled my brow earnestly. "Wouldn't a body builder with that kind of international reputation do better for himself getting some money together and putting out his own product?"

"Money is but a small part of it," Shelby said sagely. "There's a certain amount of expertise necessary for that kind of involvement. He would have to consider putting together the high-standard lab work other existing companies have, finding the necessary technicians, the pharmacists, biochemists and research people. Plus the ultimate ingredient, of course, getting your product out to the best places for sales, which we call marketing."

Shelby had a few years on me and I thought it best to humor his technological wisdom. "In other words, you're telling me he'd be smarter shooting for less. Letting experience handle it."

"To that general effect," Shelby said. After a pause he added, "Matter of fact, it may not be common knowledge, but Felix Witter had rather grandiose plans of his own after he had won his first two big contests. Thought he would start up his own company and outdo the only weight man who ever made a success of the business."

"You're referring to Johnny Albany?"

Shelby nodded. "What Felix didn't understand was that Mr. Albany is innately shrewd, and there was more to him than his muscular development." He shook his head gently as he sorrowed over the memory. "I'm afraid he lost quite a bit of money in starting his own place before realizing he was in over his depth."

"When was this, Mr. Shelby?"

His bright-blue eyes bored into mine with a laserlike zap. "As I said, after he had been chosen the best in those earlier contests. Several years ago."

It could have accounted for some of the bundle Marilyn Channing dropped on Witter, for a lot of things. "He had his own lab people—went that far?"

Another cursory nod from Shelby, who politely didn't yawn in my face. "He started, yes—discovered he couldn't hack it, and got out with his skin."

"I don't suppose you'd remember the name he was using for his company?"

Shelby looked at the ceiling but the answer wasn't there. "Sorry, no. It's escaped me."

"Perhaps you might remember who bought him out?"

Shelby regretfully wigwagged his silvery head. "Too unimportant to remember, really. Other companies in the same field, I should imagine."

"Not yours, though?"

Shelby smiled faintly. "I doubt there was enough there to warrant our interest, Mr. Roper."

"I'm interested in digging up his background to find some reason for his murder," I said. "I've already visited Johnny Albany. According to him, Witter was not particularly well-liked. I got the idea that any number of people could have been waiting for the chance to end Witter's career along with his life."

Shelby shrugged indifferently. "Even as an impartial investigator, surely you must realize that Mr. Albany had his own personal reasons. He was among the best of his time, worked very hard to get his reputation, and then Felix Witter comes along and makes hash of his achievements as well as his measurements. Mind I'm not even hinting Mr. Albany would have connived at Witter's murder. Merely to set you straight if you intend pursuing your investigation. Nearly everyone in the body-building field had good reason to want Witter dead. Simply put, he was too much competition."

Smiling, I said, "But certainly no threat to you."

Shelby rolled his eyes at the notion. "Good heavens, no!"

"I've heard Witter was involved with a lot of women with terrific crushes on him. It's been suggested there was enough competition between his castoffs and his working stable to limit the inquiry right there. Maybe you don't know it, but when it comes down to murder, women are statistically right up there with the menfolks."

"Is that a fact?" Shelby said coolly. "Well, then, in your situation, I'd certainly have to consider them, too. Although it seems to me the manner of his death would by its particular unique nature preclude a great many of your suspects. He died of strangulation, wasn't that it?"

"Induced by the substitution of a poisonous body oil for his own, containing potent amounts of an insecticide paralyzing his nervous system."

"Was that it?" Shelby murmured. "Rather a grotesque mind at work there."

"But an efficient one. A person who knew poisons and their effect on the human system. Witter might have had the greatest body in the world, but with his pores closed, he couldn't breathe. Strangulation and subsequent heart failure was just the medical examiner's own kind of shorthand."

Shelby sat shaking his head, clasping and unclasping his strong supple hands. "I believe you're suggesting now that a scientific mind, a trained biochemist, might have conceived the idea. Would that explain why you're here?"

"Not necessarily," I said. "Rat poisons and insecticides are available to anyone. Of course, if you happened to know of some particular biochemist who hated Felix Witter enough—"

"Well, I'm genuinely sorry I can't help you there," he said, sounding genuinely apathetic. He glanced at his appointment pad and moved his telephone closer. "Would there be anything else?"

"One last question, Mr. Shelby, and I'm gone. Regarding the Felix Witter line—I know Johnny Albany and his Healthfare Organics company did the manufacturing and selling of the product. But I also understand Felix Witter did the real sell himself, with his promotional tours and personal appearances. Is it possible that somebody in your employ had a personal interest in ordering and purchasing his stuff?"

"Well, hardly," Shelby said frostily. "I do all the buying. Thanks for dropping by, Mr. Roper, and I wish you luck with your inquiry."

He stood up then, elegantly imperturbable, extending his hand. With a simple handshake he got rid of me, the tie-up between Debbie Hill and Felix Witter, and Johnny Albany's allegation that he hated Witter's guts for cutting him out with her.

I left Good Earth Things wondering if Titus Shelby had a butler.

Twelve

I wondered if his executioners had persuaded our agent Dill to elaborate about my involvement with the current drug scene. That would have accounted for the Mafia-type song-and-dance men Lew and Charley who had called and wanted me to come along. The thought of my being in a men's hair salon was bad enough for my image, but the subsequent picture of being stuck under Dante's metallic hair drier while being charged with electricity soured my normal acid-free digestion.

I checked with the office to find out if Parson had called again. He hadn't. I asked if there were any calls or messages for me. There weren't. I inquired of Miss Troy if she happened to have a free evening wherein we could discuss old times and perhaps new beginnings. A teeny weeny little-girl giggle is just that much better than being laughed off outright.

"Maybe on my birthday," she said at last.

"When would that be, Miss Troy?"

"I'll let you know."

The telephone directory had all the numbers for Kay Morrow, the ex–Mrs. Felix Witter. Johnny Albany had mentioned smart money for her last known bag. It seemed an occupational hazard a young well-stacked type might easily settle for and find difficult to get out of.

The apartment was in Westwood on Beverly Glen south of

Wilshire, among the newer condominiums blighting the old high-tiered curving street. It wasn't hard to find a parking place if you didn't mind using a lot of the sidewalk. The mailbox below gave me the number, and the rising stone steps reaching toward the sky showed me the direction. Apartment nests were strung at higher recessed levels.

As I neared the last clutter of steps leading toward her eyrie, a man came down synchronized with the sound of a slamming door. He looked about my size but had a few years to spare, swarthy and good-looking, wearing expensive threads, and his eyes were black, snapping and not at all happy. He had a thin scar running alongside his jaw that had healed a long time ago but wouldn't go away. He looked like what smart money tends to look like, and his scar told me he hadn't been smart enough.

His type fitted any of the in-groups up at Vegas, or that of a minor lieutenant working for some local war lord. He had either been up and down this route before, or was a natural at running down a precipitous jagged incline. He went past me without a word, eyes taking me in without expression, and continued his breakneck jogging descent with no change of pace. His tailor had to be up there with the best, too, because the gun he carried under his left lapel merely bulged without leaving a wrinkle. I recognized him as Pete Tully, an itinerant hood.

She answered the bell ring at apartment 10 E with angry blue eyes and a terrific figure. She noticed almost immediately that I wasn't the guy dipsy-doing down all those steps, and her face relaxed, helping her become just another pretty doll.

I asked her if she was Kay Morrow and she admitted she was, shared my secret about being Max Roper, showed her the little brass buzzer and the small type in the folding wallet which certified I was a detective, and asked the usual question about coming in to ask her a few questions if she didn't mind.

She hesitated, uncertain as to whether she really did or not. They usually ask then what it's about, which is a tough one to get by, because if you tell them, they tend to slam the door in your face.

I took a chance on her having been a nice girl at one time in her life, pleasant, relating to men, not averse to small incriminating talk. "It's about the murder of Felix Witter," I confided.

She took her hand off the door edge, let it swing open, and allowed me to pass. She was wearing some special fragrance that didn't cost more than ninety-five bucks an ounce, and a brief tight-fitting dress that had to go for a C note per inch. Her hair was long and blond, and she looked as the girl next door wanted to look and then found out life wasn't going to be all that easy.

"The cops already been here," she said tonelessly. "The same day. I told them Felix and I broke up five years ago, so how did I know what's happening to him now? You want me to, I can tell you the same thing. Or maybe you got another kind of question."

"In fact, I do. Why do you live on top of so many steps?"

She noticed my heaving chest. "It's good for privacy. You'd be surprised how many deadbeats those steps eliminate. If they come back, I know they got to be serious about me."

"One passed me on the way," I said. "He looked very serious."

She pushed back her hair. "Oh, him, yeah. Well, that's tough."

"He seemed to be in great shape," I said. "He could probably turn around and run right up here again. Maybe he wouldn't like the idea of your talking to me."

"That's tough, too," she said. "Meanwhile this is still my apartment, and if he don't like it, he can get lost." She thought it over, then walked lithely to the door and closed it. "Let him worry about that, too," she said defiantly.

She came back swinging her hips without trying to excite me, her legs as good as any beauty queen's, past, current or in the hereafter. I could understand and sympathize with Johnny Albany's bereavement if she had indeed gone out of his life.

"I'll make it fast," I said. "No need to stir up the man. Is he from Vegas?"

She sat back on the sofa, crossed one beautiful leg over the other, looked up at me stonily, then smiled. "What's your next question? I thought this was going to be all about Felix."

"It is. But your friend looked like a hard type. We're talking about murder, and generally that takes in the hard types. We still don't know, for example, why Felix was killed."

"Look," she said, "if my hard-type friend, as you call him, wanted something bad to happen to Felix, it wouldn't happen in a crowded room with a lot of cruddy over-sized stiffs with muscles out to here. If you're some kind of detective, you oughtta know hard types work different. For one, they don't like to work in crowded rooms. For another, there would be more holes in Felix than you wanted to count."

I showed her I could turn my hands over, palms up. "Okay, so maybe Felix wasn't killed by this particular kind of hard type. The first question always is why—"

"Why? Because he was a no-good sonofabitch, is why. Anybody been around Felix Witter long enough to have just met him would tell you the same. Come on, now, Mr. Detective, don't make him out to be a sweet type just because he paraded all that beef around into Mr. This-and-that."

"Maybe you can tell me what happened," I said. "You were married, you must have been in love with the guy at one time."

"Sure I was. Ten years ago I was a lot dumber than I am now. He was beautiful and made my heart dance, and it was love at first sight, like they say. The greatest since Adam and Eve. Then I found out I wasn't the only girl who was crazy about him. That wouldn't have been so bad, but my guy couldn't say no. It didn't take too long before he was even looking so he couldn't say no. You take that kind of crap day after day, a couple years, and I don't care how much love you started out with, one day it's all gone. Out the window. Finished."

"Finished how long ago?" I said.

She remembered without having to check her notes. "Five years. That was just before he started to make it big. I was dumb enough to let him sweet-talk me into a nickel-and-dime settlement. The next year he won Mr. America, Mr. World and Mr. Europe. He made over a hundred grand.

"Meanwhile I was singing in little clubs, fighting off the johns and the creeps, trying to put my head together and forget the bastard." Her eyes stared out the window and her palms rubbed together. "When you sing in saloons, you think you're selling them a song. But you're just kidding yourself. They're around you to look, not to listen. And while they're looking, and you're trying for something a little different, changing key, trying to come in a fourth higher for a startling particular sound, they're thinking the same old thing: How can I get this broad into the sack?"

"Try to look at it our way," I said winningly. "You're a very attractive girl."

"Yeah," she said flatly. "So I heard."

"I'm sorry I never got the chance to see you work. I might have wanted to listen, too."

"Sure you would," she said. "Then after you listened for a while, you'd start thinking."

"I suppose," I said. "Are you still in it—working clubs? Maybe—"

"I just come back from Vegas, I don't work too often. I got my little boy to take care of. He's in school . . . and yeah, he's Felix's."

"Did he see the boy?"

"Yeah, a little, at first. Later it became a drag. He was too busy showing off the muscles."

"What about child support?"

"You kidding? From *him?* No, with Felix, it was either all or nothing. So at first I got the all, and wound up with the nothing." She smiled. "But at least it was a big nothing."

I wagged my thumb toward the world outside. "Your friend seems to have things going all right. Maybe that's something."

"Who, Pete? Well, now, he thinks he owns me. Or maybe right now he ain't so sure. It don't matter. If we split, so another guy will find me. That's one thing I can't blame on Felix. I happen to like men. It's like a curse with me."

"It means you're a natural, healthy girl," I said. "Nothing wrong with that."

She brooded. "Yeah, only I got the habit of picking the bad eggs. Know what I mean?"

I nodded. "Maybe someday," I said cheerfully, "you'll find Mr. Right."

She shook her head. "Jesus, I can't stand that type. The reformers, you mean? No, I guess I swing the other way—maybe it's the excitement."

I still had the notion that some of the excitement might be remembering something and come loping up all those steps again, just to make sure. She sounded cocky and tough, but I sensed her fear. "It's been nice talking to you. Can you think of anybody seriously who might have hated Felix just enough to kill him?"

Her eyes sparkled and she seemed to come to life. "You said 'seriously'? Jesus, maybe you think I was kidding around. Honest to God, I can't think of anybody who wouldn't have wanted to put an end to Mr. Universe-three-times."

"Wanted to is one thing. Let's narrow it down a little. Maybe you can think of someone who actually could."

She shook her head. "No way. Who knows who would or who could? He was a big strong guy, but he ain't the only one around who can dead-lift over five hundred pounds. There's a lot of other champs still around, you know, plus a lot of ex-ones who still ain't exactly invalids. I'll tell you one thing, because I been around: weight men don't get upset too easy, but you cross one and he'll remember. If he can drop a ton on your chest, he'll do it."

I nodded. "How about Johnny Albany? Would you say that he and Felix were friends or not?"

Mentioning his name didn't send her off into a swoon. "Johnny didn't like Felix no more than anybody else. But he had a use for him in his business, so he used him. You ask me, did Johnny Albany kill him, I'd have to say no."

"Why?"

"Simple. Felix was still helping him make a buck, and one thing Johnny don't turn away from is the buck. So now he'll have to try to latch on to the new one, Eddie Blue, and it won't be easy. Because Eddie Blue ain't no dope like my Felix, and

Johnny will have to show what's going on and not try to screw him around with the figures."

"Maybe Eddie Blue liked money, too," I said. "With Felix out of the way, he can cash in on his new Mr. Universe title. Maybe he's a sweet guy, but if he's good at the numbers, as you say, it would have been worth his while to ease Felix out."

"Jesus," she said. "What a mind! The way you go about it, you're suspicious of everybody."

"You go by motives in murder. Somebody stands to gain or it's revenge, with somebody trying to get even. This one was carefully planned, obviously by somebody who knew Felix well and his daily routine and training habits."

Her right eye was developing a nervous tic, and her hands were restless, moving across her body, playing with her hair. I had the notion it was a little anxiety about the hood who had just left, rather than the discussion about murder methods.

I said, "You know how Felix was killed, don't you?"

"Yeah. The leader of the fuzz filled me in. It still sounds like a freak accident to me. What if it hadn't worked?"

"That's something we may never know. Whoever planned it knew where Felix kept his body oil and his gym bag. I don't suppose you'd remember after all these years."

She was on her feet instantly, eyes hard and stormy. Her thumb showed me where the door was. "You're cute. Now do me a favor and get the hell outta here."

I got up too. "I didn't mean it that way. You might have dropped the information accidentally and somebody picked it up. Maybe you ought to think about it."

"I already did. Get lost."

She didn't change her mind and try to kiss me goodbye. I trundled down the long series of levels and steps to the street. Pete, the hard type, wasn't on his way up again, nor waiting at the bottom. So far, I had to admit, this hadn't been a real bad day.

I got into my heap and drove away from that part of Westwood wondering how a guy could look as good as Felix

Witter and have so many people hate him that much. I had a sudden flash of insight that when I found just one person who loved Witter, I'd have the killer.

I hoped it wouldn't be his mother.

Thirteen

The banks along Wilshire in Beverly Hills don't get stuck up all that much and use their time instead putting up big office buildings on most of the corners. Frank Channing had his investment-broker offices in one of them. The elevator didn't bother asking questions, trusting you could read buttons.

The reception room was a return to the womb, discreetly lit, warm and expensively carpeted. There were sporting prints on the oak-paneled walls, soft leather chairs, a Queen Anne table dotted with the latest financial mags, and a blonde behind the reception desk who looked worth the money.

I told her I was George Wilson and related the sad news of Aunt Sarah suddenly going to that big rehabilitation center in the sky before leaving me all that money. I needed sound financial advice now, I explained, to be able to invest wisely protected against the perils of inflation and unjust taxes on the wealthy. The blonde nodded sympathetically, asked me to take a seat and stood up smoothing her little skirt over her hips, illustrating better ways to invest my money. Then she trustingly left me alone with the office furniture and slithered through a door. She came back shortly, smiling fondly. Mr. Channing would be happy to see me if I cared to walk her way.

There had to be a benign planet in transit this day setting up all these sensational-looking broads for my pleasure, and I watched the curvy blonde all the way to see that she didn't pull a knife on me. I switched off as we approached Frank Channing's door, reserving some concentration for the interview, wondering how I could trick him into admitting he had knocked off Felix Witter out of love for his departed ex, Marilyn, the green-eyed sexpot. This done, I could get off the body-builder case and get back on my own track of being the prize dope in the current narcotics operation.

The stacked blond receptionist pressed my elbow indiscreetly, if Aunt Sarah's money wasn't her object. "Good luck, Mr. Wilson," she murmured. "I hope you have a pleasant stay in town. My name is Pamela May, if you have any further problems."

Channing had his hand stuck out for my money, but I shook it instead to impress him with my cautious nature. His grip was so light that I didn't realize his hand was gone until I saw it lighting a cigarette. He was a small man who looked capable of handling all the world's money. He was pressing sixty, showing close-cropped silver hair, and more intelligence than I cared to match. His black eyes were alert and shrewd, although ostensibly he didn't know beans about women and how big beautiful body builders could scramble their heads, hormonal systems and checking accounts.

His voice was a running current of well-modulated words and phrases that lapped over you like the tide. I cut in to recite the babble of my windfall inheritance. Channing nodded, but didn't leap up to lock the door and put a gun to my head.

"We're here to advise you, of course," he said, "but over the years we have found it pays to listen to our clients' own ideas. Whenever possible, if they are sound, we work toward the same end, thereby ensuring him of a continuing interest in his investment and his future."

"Well," I said uncertainly, "what I'd like to do with my money is to do something for the world, or my country, anyway . . ."

"Now, Mr. Wilson—" he said.

"I'd like to see all the kids healthy, and their mommies and daddies, too. So what I was thinking of was the health-food business. You know, like—"

"Yes, I'm familiar with the health-food business." Channing sighed, stubbed out his butt and tried a fresh one out of the deck blind. "Admittedly it's getting bigger, but there's a lot more competition, and so for the profit percentage—"

"Well, I don't care a hang about that so much—do I?"

Channing nodded brusquely. "Indeed you do, sir. Because otherwise your business won't be able to cope with rising costs. Perhaps we can suggest some other facets for your money, while keeping in mind your altruistic intent of benefiting the world."

"I don't know," I said. "I went to one of those big muscle shows a while ago that you people were putting on down here. I saw what some of those men looked like. You know, they all were like Greek gods, and that's a fact, Mr. Channing. And they all said they owed it all to those little bottles of vitamins and minerals and what-not. So I thought, if they could do it, then I could do it. If I could get a lot of kids to look like that, I'd be happy. I know Aunt Sarah would."

"I'm sure she would, but let's be sensible for a moment, Mr. Wilson. For one thing, those men who looked like Greek gods to you had to work and train very hard for their muscular development. They didn't get it from what was in those precious little bottles you mentioned."

I showed surprise. "They didn't? But they claimed—"

Channing smiled. "Advertising, Mr. Wilson. Surely you've heard of that? The manufacturer pays a certain amount to the athlete for his testimonial. It helps to sell his product."

"That doesn't sound honest to me," I said. "Now, you take that fellow who won most of the titles. That big blond guy who suddenly fell over dead while performing—what was his name?"

Channing looked bland. "I don't know. I don't follow those things. About how much money were you considering for investment purposes, Mr. Wilson?"

"All of it, I guess," I said. "But naturally, I'm here to take your advice. The only thing is, you see, I've got this stubborn streak, and so while I admit you know what's best, I still would like to know why my idea is so far out. What I'm trying to say is, is there any way you can show me in black-and-white figures that this health-food business and profit is bad as you say for me?"

Channing didn't look any sadder than you'd expect. "Yes, if you're that interested, I guess we can get their volume, gross and net earnings for you. Take a while, you understand. There are over a dozen big companies we'd have to check out."

"Fine," I said. "I went through a couple of those health stores before dropping in on you. There's one fellow used to be a big titleholder himself. Mr. America, I think. Got his name and picture on the bottle. He looked mighty good, Mr. Channing, and the salesclerk there told me what's in that bottle checks out—that it really works."

"Well," Channing said, sinking lower in his chair.

I snapped my fingers. "Johnny Albany. That's his name. And the other chap, the one who just died, he's got a pretty good line out himself. Now, don't you think that a lot of kids are seeing those pictures of these champions looking so great, and would want to take the stuff themselves?"

"I doubt it seriously, Mr. Wilson. For one thing, the youngsters aren't doing the shopping in those stores, but rather the adults. For another, if you're interested in taking my advice, I can think of several companies right at this moment, that can use a little extra capital, and give you a chance to double your money within the year, with built-in deferment clauses to negate any possible income tax payments for several years. How much did you say your aunt had left you?"

I shrugged. "A couple million."

Channing sat up better and tried a new butt from a fancy pack. "With that kind of investment, you could buy half a company, with preferred stock deals that nobody could touch. I'd suggest you think about that, but we'll go ahead and get those other figures for you, if you insist."

I nodded my cornball head. "There's something else about that business. Did you ever get a look at some of the women these muscle men have?"

"Frankly, no," Channing said smoothly. "They're a bit out of my line."

"Well, I have, and take my word for it, they're all so beautiful you wouldn't believe it. You want to get a look at some real splendid examples of womanhood, Mr. Channing, you should go to some of those body-builder shows."

Channing was smiling when he rose from his chair. He let me touch his soft hand fleetingly again. "Beautiful women are no problem, Mr. Wilson. Granted, there are a lot of them out there, but I'd be disappointed to hear that you think the trick to getting them is by having big muscles." He shook his head wisely. "You already have the trick—waiting to be put to use sensibly. It's called money. More women like money than muscles, Mr. Wilson."

I looked as if the thought had never come my way.

He patted my back and led me toward his door. "Offhand I can think of fifty ways to double your money. As for the women, we wouldn't have to touch your capital at all. The interest alone can get you more beautiful women than you can expect to use in your lifetime."

He showed me out then, still suave, cool, leaving me with the distinct impression that replacing his dear departed wife presented him with no problems. Witter, obviously, meant nothing to him, and murder had to be far from his thoughts.

I remembered Marilyn Channing warmly as one of the better sexpots around; the kind who simply respond to men and money cuts no ice at all. Channing apparently had his own formula for the game. If he lost one, he could afford another, but I had to think that possibly at his age, the sex drive wasn't all that important, and perhaps he wanted women merely for their decorative value, and wasn't, strictly speaking, hungering.

The moneymaking instinct is a different kind of hunger, linked with power drives and eliminating emotional hangups. If Frank Channing had killed Felix Witter, it would have been done only because his wife's fancy for the gorgeous body builder was too expensive a habit. It didn't figure, though, because he seemed to have more than enough left. But then, you never know.

The blonde at the reception desk handed me a slip of paper as I passed, and hoped that I had a nice day. They say that a lot in L.A. without much heart behind it. But I assumed the numbers she had scribbled down were for her home phone, and I could tell the girl had genuine warmth.

I was shedding my millions as I went out the door, feeling, as we all do when we lose our dough, that you really don't have a friend you can depend on.

But I thought my interview, while not up to Academy performance standards, had been satisfying. Frank Channing was the first I had met who professed not to hate Felix Witter. There was the possibility he was a better actor than I thought, his investment-broker line was all a front while he went about his real business of knocking off his wife's lovers.

Fourteen

San Francisco isn't a bad town if you're not face down on a dark side street with three or four hard guys trying to kick your ribs out of your skin. It has the pulsing culture of a civilized city, a lot of good clubs and restaurants, and beautiful women.

Across the Oakland bridge is the University of California at Berkeley, where the kids first started to think about the world they were living in, where the girls liberated bras, and where Dr. Freddie Guest played with biofeedback. He was the professor Debbie Hill had told me Felix Witter had been jealous of. I knew a little about the positive aspects of the new science of biofeedback, how subjects can be trained to alter their normal unconscious body processes, slow or speed up their heart rate, reduce their blood pressure, find hidden pleasure sites in their brains, relate them with alpha and theta rhythms and thereby learn to do away with girls. That didn't interest me nearly as much as meeting somebody like Guest who could disturb Witter, chosen many times over as the undisputed best in the world.

The ride over the bridge is more exciting than the college town. But the kids are hip and crazy and if you don't get stopped too often to sign petitions, you can get to like it.

The very attractive young black girl at the registration desk inside the administration building showed me a big smile and a lot of satiny thigh as she spun sideways to check her psycho-physiology-class schedules. She was shapely enough to make me forget why I wanted to spend time talking with Freddie Guest, but she dug out the sheet and explained Professor Guest wasn't on this day, and probably could be reached at home. She sensed I was the follow-up type but wrote down his home phone and address instead of hers.

I called but the phone kept on ringing. I decided to ease my rented Mustang over there and take the chance he was out in his garden trying biofeedback on his plants. The ride out was scenic and so was the street where Professor Guest lived. Huge pines and old Victorian houses. I found his, a small cottage with an untrimmed lawn, and knocked on his door. He didn't answer and I went around the side to the rear.

He had a vegetable garden patch that looked healthy and blooming, but the translator wasn't around for them to explain how they did it. I tried the rear door. It was open and I walked through his kitchen and living room. He didn't answer my hearty calls but I heard water running and went upstairs.

He was in the bathroom shower but with that kind of bullet hole in his head, I knew he wasn't coming out to dry himself and talk. His body was cold. It could have been the cold water, or he had been killed long enough for him to cool off. I was the detective but I didn't know.

His bedroom had nothing more going for it than a narrow bed, an old bureau with opened drawers and flaking paint, a tattered throw rug and a cracked paint-starved ceiling. Any romantic elements there would have had to be by the grace of God and the imaginations of interested parties.

His study downstairs was small and about as threadbare. A small desk, an old wooden filing cabinet, raw-wood bookshelves resting on bricks. Books were thrown around and the desk and file cabinet drawers were open, suggestions even to a dull-wit detective that somebody was looking for something.

It could have been the professor upstairs who might have hidden his soap and not been able to find it again, but I had to doubt it. There were notebooks on his desk, and I flipped through them all without finding any more clues to his murder than his listing of experiments in the biofeedback line. According to what I read, rats were about as good as humans in finding their pleasure centers, but I thought everybody already knew that.

The killer hadn't left any cute calling cards. No stick figures signed SCORPIO or TAURUS or any such known random thrill killers. He didn't leave a picture of himself or a thumbprint I could notice. I went through everything downstairs and then tried the kitchen, and on a top shelf between the corn starch and the lentil beans I found an opened coffee can with fifty thousand dollars' worth of crisp bills in it. I knew biofeedback people weren't accustomed to having that much ready cash around. I called the police to fill them in on the dire doings on Spruce Street, and left trying to think.

The excitingly shapely young black-skinned girl in the school building had been replaced by a chunky solid Nordic type with tremendous boobs and a vacant stare to go with them. I lasered her with my best eye and found her concentration core. That led me down the hall and into a large office where the head of the psychophysiology department, Dr. Walter Holt, was leaning on his elbows.

I told him who I was and explained why I was there to interrupt his afternoon nod. I asked if he knew of any enemies Professor Guest had, other than the rats, cats and humans he had curarized before pasting electrodes on their skulls to check their EEG brain-wave patterns.

Dr. Holt was shocked first to learn that he had to find another tenant to sublet his house on Spruce Street to. Guest was a quiet, steady person, he said, not given to wild parties, lived pretty much to himself, and wasn't given to throwing the furniture around. He had been at the university for three years, was thirty-two years old, and never behind in his rent. He was a specialist in the biofeedback game and lately his experiments had led to discovery of new brain rhythms in cats.

"Sensorimotor rhythms," Holt explained. "From the sensory and motor areas of the cortex. Twelve to sixteen cycles per second."

"What does it do?" I said.

"They become motionless, take odd and rigid postures, and somehow can then ward off the effects of drugs and poisonous compounds."

Professor Guest's murderer obviously had to be either a cat lover or one who hated the purring things. It made sense for that kind of person to kill a man who was apparently developing ways for cats to avoid being poisoned by him. I suggested these alternatives to Professor Holt, who blinked and looked around for his ashtray with the dead cigar in it.

"Not very likely. Guest's experiments were not that well known," Morrow said slowly. "But what is disappointing here is that his work was cut short just as he had found the post-reenforcement rhythm."

I wondered out loud what that could be, and Holt knew. "It's to do with the pleasure centers of the brain. The cats developed a slower brain wave after getting their milk reward. This slow wave is only four to twelve cycles per second, which encompasses most of alpha and theta. The more of this rhythm the cats produced, the less they cared about their milk reward. They just lay around purring, eyes closed, in an obvious state of bliss.

"As you can imagine," Holt continued, "such training with humans could lead to profound personality changes—turning a normally tense or neurotic person into one who is fulfilled and happily disposed."

I asked if Professor Guest had received any strange visitors of late. Holt shook his head, didn't know of any. "He was a very quiet person, lived a quiet and private life. His work was his one and consuming interest."

"What about girls?" I said. "Girls, like girl students. A grown man can't have all that much fun pasting electrodes on pussycat skulls."

Dr. Holt looked skeptical. "I don't know. He was really rather fond of his cats."

I nodded to indicate I could understand that kind of ongoing obsession, but asked if I could get a list of his classes and students. Dr. Holt frowned and didn't think that should be necessary. Student rights, he explained. One had to be extremely careful.

I reminded him we were talking about murder.

He pushed back his glasses. "Well, yes, but we've just about rebuilt all the labs they destroyed last year. We wouldn't want to stir them up again."

I asked if he had in mind any replacement for young Professor Guest. "We may by-pass the program temporarily," he said. "Perhaps consider other ideas of altering states of consciousness. Or we may go into advanced studies of nutrition."

"Nutrition," I said.

He nodded. "Perhaps combined with organic gardening. A great many of our young people are adopting AmerIndian methods with food and the soil. A closer identification with nature. They should know the scientific findings about proper nutrition before they reject their own culture completely and irrationally."

I didn't want to find out the Great Spirit had been bamboozling the Indians all these years, and left him alone with his dead cigar. I went back to the registration desk. The bovine blonde was still on her seat.

I showed her the brass L.A. buzzer and a lot of authority, talked fast and she thought the FBI had landed. She found the file cabinet with the folders on class registrants and allowed me to take down the names of Professor Guest's dozen students. When she thought of asking why the FBI needed their names, I explained how the government was making big decisions on grants for advanced learning, and the biofeedback kids were the most likely to hear from Santa Claus early. She thanked me for going to all that trouble, and I got out of there fast before Dr. Holt began his afternoon sleepwalk.

I decided to stay over for the medical examiner's report, and San Francisco had the hotels and better watering places. The St.

Francis always gets my money and they found me a nice room with a good view of the flagpole in front of Union Square.

I had the cannelloni at Paoli's and a few drinks. The town was humming but I had the wrong vibrations. I went back to the hotel, picked up a paper, a bottle and some smokes and shook off a few lovely call girls in the lobby. It wasn't quite nine o'clock, and before I began checking out some of Professor Guest's students, I fixed myself a drink and went through the paper. The Dodgers had won, Shoemaker had brought in three longshots, and the Organic Food Society had a lecture on nutrition by guest speaker Ms. Debbie Hill.

I had forgotten our tentative date, and apparently she hadn't done any worse. The lecture time was given as eight-thirty and I knew I had to be there. I red-buttoned a few elevators and the lobby downstairs had a directory listing for the Organic Food Society hall. I went out faster than a hooker on the arm of a house dick and found a cab.

The lecture hall was near the Cannery at the foot of Columbus Avenue, near Beach, with a sparkling view of the Bay and San Francisco skyline. I wanted more than visual entertainment and followed the worn stone steps into the hall.

It was a packed and mixed gathering. Young and old of all the sexes interested in what the food merchants were stirring into the product, the hidden bombshells in additives, preservatives and coloring agents and dyes. You couldn't do too much about your air and water, but with food, somehow the powers guiding us had torn up the "or else" contract and given everybody a fighting chance.

The very attractive dark-haired visiting nutritionist and salesperson from L.A. was well into her talk, coming around the pole and heading into the stretch showing her expertise on the glop in gustatory lane. The audience sat quietly packed on rows of wooden chairs, following every word and line of the speaker raptly. Nobody saw me enter and I stood inside the doors cornering the room for an available and inconspicuous seat.

San Francisco is a city of surprises and I got mine when I saw a big man sitting back on the rear left aisle. I knew him as Parson, the DEA agent I thought was dead.

I recalled his last words to me concerning agent Dill had been interrupted by muffled gunshots. Drug Enforcement Administration agents tend to gather information from nark addicts and finks and are not generally disposed toward concern with good healthy organic foods.

I backed off away from his possible line, looked around and found another surprise. This one was gray-haired, chunky, stodgy and middle-aged with thick horn-rimmed glasses and a rumpled suit. I had seen him only a few hours ago sitting at his desk trying to stay awake. Even without the dead cigar, I recognized him as Dr. Walter Holt, the sleepy cautious-minded psychophysiology-department head and house renter from the university at Berkeley.

I backed out the big double entrance doors to sort things out. It was a dark night and the new Chinese restaurant across the street showed gold walls and mandarin-orange drapes through its peekaboo window glass. I lit up a butt and a car came around the corner from Beach and stopped in front of the hall.

Two men stepped out. Lectures on food were bigger than I had thought. The men headed for the steps and looked familiar, but I wasn't sure until the smaller one in front showed me his gun. It was an expensive model recommended by law authorities.

"Okay, Roper. Let's go."

The bigger man behind nodded. "Unless maybe you got a way to prove that butt in your mouth ain't a butt but a new kinda land mine you just invented."

It's always good to meet old pals, and San Francisco can warm your heart with its surprises and attachments. Or otherwise, as when you meet once again your favorite vaudeville team—that Explosive Duo, fresh from their most recent pulse-pounding personal appearance, the song-and-dance killer clowns from Los Angeles—Lew and Charley.

Fifteen

"I wouldn't want to insult your intelligence, Charley," I said. "Obviously, this cigarette isn't a land mine. But nearly everybody knows cigarettes can kill you."

He wigwagged with the gun. "Get inna car."

It was a nice peaceful ride without any burdensome conversation because Charley tagged me behind the ear as I bent toward entering the car. He was very good at putting the lights out and I slept quietly until it was time to get up again.

I smelled the waterfront and it wasn't any worse than always. The car was easing slowly through a narrow dark alley and pulled up in front of a warehouse. Charley's .38 was cold and heavy on my nose.

"Okay, move it."

My skull told me it was all right, it was all healed up although hurting, and to go along. They had me double-teamed, walking the point behind my hips. The moon was shrouded in fog and I couldn't pick out a lucky star anywhere in the universe.

The warehouse was as big as a warehouse and our footsteps echoed better than any in your usual B movie. There were a lot of big wooden crates around, but so far I wasn't packed inside any of them.

The place was lit up by overhead lights and the concrete floor was as cold as it had to be. There was a small flat kitchen-type table farther down the course and a wooden kitchen chair in front of it. There wasn't any table setting, no napkins, and I couldn't smell meatballs and spaghetti coming from behind the closed office door. The menu was off at the printer's.

"Siddown," Charley said.

I took the chair, hoping the service was going to be better than Charley's impersonation of a maître d'. Charley dusted off his hands and looked up. I followed his gaze and saw a lot of bright lights pinned at the studs and rafters. Charley must have read the script because he just nodded and walked away, taking the rest of his comedy team with him. Their footsteps echoed with the same hollow sound until I couldn't hear them.

A voice spoke from somewhere above. "Hey, you, Roper."

The voice was on tape juxtaposed to a playback or he had an echo and liked it, or a mike that needed adjusting. My head swiveled, trying to pinpoint the voice, and settled for the brightest bulb in the joint.

"Lissen, Roper," the bright bulb said. "Lissen real good now."

I nodded to ease the crick in my neck that you can get sometimes from lissening real good.

"My name is Shine," the bulb said. He didn't laugh and probably didn't understand the joke. "Ya don't know me, so we keep it that way. Ya don't even try to know me and it's a lot better."

I wanted to tell him there was supposed to be an energy crisis going on, and it would help me as well as the country if he cut down a little. By squinting, I could make out some kind of human figure squarely behind the light, but I knew I could never make him out in a shape-up line at any place but a light-bulb factory.

Mr. Shine, if indeed it was he, had more to say in thunderous overtones. "Twenty-five million bucks," he orated.

"Sir?" I said, aware even then of my modest fees.

"A heist. Twenty-five mill. The white stuff—snow."

We were talking cocaine and its tangential habit.

"You find it, you live. The broad lives. Okay?"

"What broad, Mr. Shine?" I said to the upstairs gallery-and-light foundation.

"You know. Don't smartass me. The vitamin broad."

I knew but one vitamin broad, and at the moment, unless too much time had passed, she was giving her all for the sake of nutrition and sales to that small but eclectic group gathered at the Organic Food hall.

"Ya hear me, Roper?"

But there could be others. Vitamin broads here and there, San Francisco and elsewhere. It was a comparatively new field, and the women's libbers were still burgeoning, enlarging their vistas. Besides, Debbie Hill couldn't have heisted any $25 million worth of anything, let alone cocaine. Hadn't she assured me herself how straight she was?

"Ya got five days to get it up."

The Lord had done more in six, but things were easier in the old days.

"How will I know it's your stuff, Mr. Shine?"

"Good question. It ain't been cut. I'm talkin pure, dig?"

Twenty-five million dollars' worth of uncut pure would eventually bring ten times that amount going around the street. Mr. Shine had good reason for those ringing authoritative overtones. He was talking about a quarter of a billion bucks, just about the amount my life, I figured, was worth, considering the overtime put in and the attendant hazards.

"Suppose I find it, how do I get it to you?"

"No sweat. We'll keep in touch."

I thought I detected movement above on the upper landing and then footsteps, but I couldn't be sure. The bulb I had been staring at held its high voltage, blinding me. The others strung around the upper level weren't much better.

I waited for another word from Shine. He didn't seem to have any but I waited a little longer, not wishing to seem rude. My eyes hurt, my head hurt, and my neck was giving me almost as much pain as Mr. Shine.

I stood up, kicked the chair away. Nobody bellowed for me to siddown. Nobody shot any guns or threw a blade. My feet guided me back across the concrete, and my head reminded me not to bother examining the insides of any of the crates.

I found the door and stepped outside, still blinded by the lights. My comedy team materialized from the shadows and Charley stuck his gun in my ear. "Hold it, pal. We'll take you back to your hotel."

I wanted to tell him it wasn't necessary, I could find my own way, flag a cab, but Charley didn't want me to remember where the warehouse was. Either that, or he just liked to zap me over the head.

He knew my head better than I did. I woke up as the car pulled up to the side entrance of the St. Francis.

"Okay, Roper. Move your ass out."

I did that, missing the old days when gangsters had more flair and used blindfolds. The night man saw me weave through the lobby door and asked if I needed any help.

"Only in five days," I told him.

Sixteen

Back in my room, I did the best thing I knew of for a headache and nagging frustration and hit the bottle. It didn't hit back; we got along fine. I called the food fanatics' hall and the phone kept ringing. When it was answered, the impatient voice identified itself as the cleaning woman. The lecture all over, she said, everyone gone home. She hung up before I had a chance to ask if the guest speaker had passed out small plastic bags of a crystalline product to her audience to help them pick up a new habit.

I called a few hotels to find out if they registered a Ms. Debbie Hill, and they went through the motions and told me they did not. There were lots more hotels, but I cooled off. As a traveling lecturer, she could be off to another place, another town where proper diet was coming on strong over key-switching parties, or she might have gone back to L.A.

I called the constabulary in Berkeley and identified myself to their forensic man, who had a good tag for the line, Dr. Bill Blood. I offered Doc Shipman, the L.A. pathologist, as my character reference, and he loosened up and told me some of what I wanted to know.

He told me the deceased was a white male, thirty-two years old, name of Dr. Fred Guest, employed at the university. Cause of death due to gunshot wounds, homicide. Probable weapon, a .22 fired at close range. Ballistics was still on the report.

"When was he killed, Doc?"

"Approximate time of death ten A.M. to twelve noon."

"Could it have been earlier?"

"Yeah—or later. You get these bodies soaked in cold water and you never really come close. It's an educated guess and I had to put something down. The only one who could tell us for sure was the victim, and he can't talk."

"Well, there's the killer, also."

"Sure. When you catch up with him, find out for me. I'm interested for personal reasons. I'm thinking of killing my wife."

"Luck."

"Yeah. I know divorce is the more rational thing to do. But somehow killing her makes more and more sense."

I asked if they had any suspects yet on Guest's murder. So far, he told me, I was the only one.

It was an hour till midnight. Having my skull sapped twice in one night, and meeting with the light-bulb king Shine made my adrenalin flow. I got up too nervous to hang around and went out hoping I'd get a chance to hit somebody and work it off.

The North Beach part of town seemed as good a place as any and a cab tootled me over. The gay joints on Broadway were swinging and the walks were jammed with sightseers. I got out to lend them a hand.

The pictures and posters were all a come-on for the nudie shows with a little simulated sex thrown in. A lot of places had been busted and appeals were piling up. Meanwhile the street looked wide open. There were hookers on every corner, standing in doorways, with variety enough for any kind of libido. They mouthed their little whispered patter as you went by. "Hey, big boy, why do it alone? I can help you, man."

The cooking smells from some of the dives intermingled in the close night and you could develop heartburn with a few deep breaths. The street characters paraded their bizarre threads, and when that wasn't enough, boosted their images higher with six-inch wedgie platform shoes.

I found a small joint without a barker, combo or floor show and had a beer and some hot chili. There was sawdust on the floor, some still there from the day the place opened. The clientele was mostly on the quiet side: a few drunks trying to eat it off, a sniffer with the shakes, a couple of gays holding hands, heads together over the menu.

I thought about Mr. Shine and the big heist and Debbie Hill. It was like accusing a girl scout of doping the cookies. I thought about Witter and Freddie Guest and the fifty grand on his kitchen shelf, Dr. Holt and Parson, and wondered what the hell was going on.

I got out on the street and started walking. I got bumped by a lot of people, but it beat thinking. A restaurant featured Indian cuisine and looked softly lit and romantic. The menu pasted on the glass boasted of tandoori chicken, giant shrimp from Cochin, steak, curry, and exotic drinks including Pimm's Cup and other specialties. Peering through the dark glass, I saw colorfully garbed Indian and Pakistani waiters, a Sikh maître d' and Bengal-tiger skins on the walls. Beyond, the room was candlelit and at least fifty bucks a head better than my chili joint.

A man and woman came out. They looked like June and September, and in another way they looked like Debbie Hill and Dr. Holt. Either the plot was thickening or they were just two more people who had finished having dinner in an expensive and colorful joint. A cab pulled up, they got in, and neither thought of looking my way and asking me along. The cab picked up enough speed to beat the corner light and leave me guessing.

The sounds of a man and female person shouting pulled me around the corner. A small crowd had gathered to watch the show. The girl was black, young and thin, looking like a fourteen-year-old hooker. The man bulked over her, his back toward me, yelling something. The girl screamed back at him, and the big guy pulled back his hand and smashed the side of her face, knocking her against a wall. The crowd watched, as crowds do, liking the action. The man tried to pull the girl off the wall and she fought back. He slapped her again hard and I was moving closer.

The big man grabbed her wrist and started dragging her

across the sidewalk to a car parked at the curb. The kid was slapping at his hand ineffectually, calling him all those words girls know today. He had muscled her to the car and was reaching for the door handle when I tapped his broad back. It wasn't any harder than cement but I didn't care. He took his hand off the car door and swung his arm back to brush me away.

He was a big guy about six five about two fifty. I pulled his swinging arm back and gave him the turning movement and the one attacking vital spots with the arm, hitting him with a good left hook to the lower abdomen. He grunted and jackknifed forward, and my right was on its way. I recognized him as Parson a split second before my fist smashed into his broad face.

But I was all wound up, my adrenalin choking me, and let it fly. My fist established contact *(mitchaku suru)* and the big DEA man fell back over the fender and hood of his car, his nose and mouth spilling blood, his face a crimson mask, cursing.

I waited until he got his breath back and his eyes in focus. He was coming off the car at me when I held up my hand. "Sorry, Parson—I didn't recognize you."

His yellow eyes widened and he shook his head, taking me in. "Roper? What the hell was that?" He wiped blood off his smashed lip with the back of his hand, looked down at the red smear. "Sonofabitch—where the hell you get off popping me?"

I had to shrug apologetically. "I just saw the kid and some big ape whaling her." I gave him my own injured look. "It couldn't be you. The last time we talked on the phone you were being shot at—remember?"

He motioned with his hand. "Oh yeah, that . . ." His head swiveled. "Where the hell is that goddamn little tart?"

"Come on, Parson," I said soothingly, moving to block his view of the crowd. "That's not your line any more, remember?"

He glared and wagged his thick forefinger in front of my eyes. "Don't tell me my line, shamus. What's happening now is my business." He craned over my shoulder, tried to push me aside. "Outta my way. I see the little bitch!"

I shifted my feet, blocking him off, and waved my hands. "Come on, forget the kid. We got more important things to talk about—I thought you were dead!"

"That's what you'll be if you don't move it," he said, raging. He saw I was still there, grabbed my lapel and swung a long pushing blow into my chest, driving me back.

He was turning into the crowd, going after the kid, when I got back to him. I chopped him knife hand across the back of his neck, knife hand kidney blow to the right side, and brought up the same edge of my palm to the side of his neck. Parson wobbled and I added an ankle kick to the side of his knee and he went down.

I found the girl behind the ring of onlookers, crying, head back against the wall. Parson's hand prints were angry welts on her face.

"What happened?" I said.

She stopped crying every few words. "Well, yeah, I tried to hustle the bastard, but he got mad. He wanted to know who my boyfriend is, was he pushing dope. I tole him I don't have no boyfriend. He hit me and started draggin me to the car, said he was gonna beat it outta me."

I took out a bill. "Find a cab. Get off the street. He's a bad man."

"That's what they was tellin me. Now I know for sure. Thanks, mister."

A cab cruising by stopped and the kid got in. I shut the door behind her and told the cabbie to get going. Then I went back to Parson. He was on his feet again, eyes glassy, half sitting on the hood of his car. "The girl told me what happened," I said. "You've got to be out of your freaking mind. I thought you were supposed to be up here doing a job."

Parson braced his hands on the hood, shoulders bunching under his soiled coat. His voice was low, hoarse and mean. "I'll get you for this, you sonofabitch. I'll kill you for this, Roper."

I shrugged. "How about now? It's still too early to turn in."

He didn't answer, continued glaring, sucking at his breath. I turned my back on him and started away. Somebody in the crowd cried out, but I heard his rush, anyway. I moved one step to the side as advocated by Professor Takahashi Hamakichi, Eighth Dan of the Kodokan in Tokyo, my old judoka instructor. I gave Parson side high kick *(yoko-keage),* catching him squarely under his chin. It stopped his rush cold, lifted him a foot in the San Francisco night air, and knocked him back flat over the hood of his car.

I could have followed up and killed him, but I wasn't that mad. Besides, I figured that could wait until I saw Parson again and found out what happened to my friend, agent Dill.

Seventeen

Shine said five days.

Five days is a lot of days if you're in the sack with a love bird who won't quit. A lot of days if you're somewhere in the Pacific on a rubber raft beating off sharks, lost in the woods or married to a nag.

It's not that many if you're looking for a heisted powder that gets cut six to ten ways and moves fast along the street. Not many if your health is tied up with end results. Not if your best suspect is improbable, a lady vitamin pusher.

Although Shine's traveling enforcement team of Lew and Charley weren't too bright, they carried all the equipment they needed to punch holes in people. And if they got sloppy and careless, I had no doubt Shine had other entertainers in his employ.

Marilyn Channing was a provocative, sexy dish, and finding Felix Witter's killer for her seemed a likely way of ensuring another shot at her along with her expandable checkbook. But I didn't need a go with an astrologer to tell me staying alive was a more immediate concern, more in keeping with my life style of continuing to read the Sunday funnies.

The biofeedback prof's murder was a job for the locals. Dr. Holt's seeming enchantment with Debbie Hill was understandable, but his problem. Whatever the discarded people in Felix

Witter's life had in for him could wait. He was dead now and couldn't walk over anybody any more. If he was the bastard they claimed, he deserved to be dead, and so it made all kinds of sense to disengage myself from that jigsaw puzzle.

But the fifty thousand big ones in Professor Guest's coffee can bothered me. That kind of stand-by loot was strictly unbecoming to a biofeedback merchant. It made better sense if he had outguessed the bookies a couple of times at the track, ran the local numbers racket, moonlighted abortions, or had some kind of a good run at the Vegas tables.

The fifty grand suggested instead payola or payoff money. For goods received in top condition, or for goods in transit payable on delivery. Dealing with narcotics could bring that kind of money into a man's kitchen, and very possibly kill him in the end.

But Shine never mentioned Professor Guest. The vitamin broad, he said.

I hopped the early morning plane back to L.A., hoping to find her alive, friendly and willing to discuss all angles of this very strange turn of events. I called her at her apartment and nobody answered. The Good Earth Things switchboard girl said sorry, but Miss Hill hadn't come in yet. I drove over to her Marina del Rey apartment, hoping she might still be recognizable.

It was a shade before noon and nearly all the swinging singles in that play area had already left for work. Ringing her doorbell didn't bring any response, and unlike easier mysteries her door remained locked. It seemed a good bet that Miss Hill had other commitments and still hadn't returned to her pad.

But with Shine pointing the finger at her, I had to be sure.

The manager of the apartment complex couldn't remember if Miss Hill had come and gone earlier, and added that it wasn't any of his business. Also, Miss Hill was a new tenant and he wasn't at all certain as to her nocturnal or diurnal patterns. Since he was so familiar with the English language and its niceties, I threw in the one I knew about.

"Murdered? Here?" he squeaked.

"It's a possibility. Miss Hill is unfortunate enough to have a look-alike with a criminal record, and we've been given a tip her life may be in danger."

The manager got to his feet then, found his keys, and led me back to her door. "Most irregular, this," he said, putting his house key in the slot after cautiously sounding her bell a few times.

The door opened and the manager cleared his throat and tried her name a time or two, then shrugging, advanced farther into the dark apartment. He stopped suddenly, muttered, "Good heavens! You may be right, sir!"

He was referring to the condition of the rooms. The furniture had been upended and zealously taken apart, rugs cut and turned back. Dresser drawers and bookshelves emptied on the floor.

Her bedroom didn't reveal any body but did show the same dedication toward a thorough search. The bathroom didn't have anything more sickening in it than a dissolving cake of soap in the basin. Under it were damp pink panties.

"Well," he said with agitation, "at least it would seem Miss Hill is unharmed. But did you ever see such a mess? Whatever could they have been looking for?"

I thought I knew. "The look-alike I told you about had stolen a large amount of valuable jewelry," I said. "Obviously they shook down the place looking for it. They wasted their time, of course, as the police have the actual hideout staked out."

"My word!" he said. "Don't you think they should know about this?"

I shrugged indifferently. "I'll report it as soon as I get back. They'll certainly appreciate your cooperation."

He mopped his head. "But who's going to pay for this? It's an outrage!"

"No problem. Just fix it up and send them your bill."

"Well," he said, "that's a bit better, isn't it?"

I nodded. "Send it to the attention of Lieutenant Camino of Homicide West. He's very good at making good on citizens' claims."

"Wonderful, wonderful," he said. "And may I have your name, sir, for my records?"

"Witter," I said. "Detective Felix Witter. Camino knows Miss Hill is innocent of any wrongdoing, so it will be no problem."

I went around again to make sure that whoever had taken Debbie Hill's pad apart hadn't missed the stash of the $25 million coke heist. I checked under the basin, under the toilet lid. There wasn't anything like little glassine envelopes used by stamp dealers, with flaky stuff, inside her shoes in the closet, and no empty coffee cans on her kitchen shelves. The manager nervously asked me what I was looking for, and I told him. Fingerprints.

There wasn't a sign in her closet of the dress she had worn in San Francisco. No suitcase, no matchbook cover of the snazzy Punjabi Indian restaurant. The manager was thanking me profusely when I left, locking her apartment door again.

I tootled toward the streets of Venice nearby, where there were junkies who might know more than I did. Somewhere along the line of contact man, pusher and buyer, word could have dropped of the Great Cocaine haul.

Cocaine is called coke, heaven dust, star dust, the flaky stuff, the girl and God. The Peruvian Indians, who ought to know, say that God is a substance. They say it about coca, the leaf they chew, and about 90 percent of the Andes Indians are users.

The leaf comes off the bush *Erythoxylon coca*, grown on terraced ground or upland mountain slopes in Bolivia and Peru. The Indians in the high altitudes of the Andes region perform heavy labor in addition to the long treks and climbs, and like the leaf for its appetite-depressant and stimulant effects. They chew their leaves mixed with a lime alkali from bricks of pressed ashes, from quinoa, a local pigweed, adding cornstarch for adhesion or wrapped around the guano of bird droppings. Saliva acts with the alkali to release the cocaine from the leaves.

It's been consumed for centuries by the Andes Indians and is not considered to be a dangerous drug abuse there but rather similar to coffee drinking elsewhere. The Indian chewing his two ounces of leaf takes about seven-tenths grain of cocaine daily. The cocaine addict consumes from 6 to 8 grains a day, sometimes needing the bite of the bittersweet stuff and its temporary euphoria every ten minutes.

Cocaine loses potency taken by mouth, and is usually sniffed or injected. It acts upon the central nervous system with hyperstimulation and hallucinatory experiences. When taken in the small doses of the habitual user, as much as 10 grains are ingested daily. A single dose of 1.2 grains (1,200 milligrams) can be an o.d. and lethal to most humans.

Cocaine is unlike other hard drugs in that the body develops no particular tolerance to it. Even after long-term use, the same ingestion begets a similiar effect and the lethal dosage remains the same. When the drug's effect of elation and heightened physical mental and physical powers wanes, a corresponding depression sets in, the user misses his previous high and so becomes psychically dependent on the stuff.

It's fairly easy to spot the users because they're either anemic from its appetite-depressant effects or they have too many skin abscesses from injecting. The sniffers who snort snow run the risk of losing the partition between their nostrils, the lining of the nose, and the nose itself. The bone deteriorates as the blood vessels in the nasal septum constrict, followed by necrosis, perforation and infection, and the partition wears away.

A lot of the cocaine shooters like to mix it with heroin, making it a "speedball." The euphoria of the two drugs taken together is greater than that of either one, and the heroin helps to prolong the effect as well as smooth down the rough edges of the cocaine. With an amphetamine, it becomes a *bombita*.

Dr. Sigmund Freud made the first detailed study of the physiological effects of cocaine, and felt the drug could be used as a cure for morphine addiction. He tried the cure on another doctor, cured the morphine addiction, and produced the first documented cocaine addict. Later, Freud developed the habit himself, which goes to prove something or other.

I zeroed in on the first gray-green junkie on the street. He looked to be a coke head with his habit coming down and I hustled him fast before his symptoms shook him out of sight.

I showed him a tenner. "This is for anything you can tell me about a big operation around town lately."

His hand fastened greedily on the bill. "What kinda operation, Charlie?"

"Big snow heist."

He shook his head sadly, eyes tearful. "Sorry, Dave. I don't know nothin on that."

I didn't want to influence his character. "Maybe you might know somebody who knows."

He sighed, his breath rattling in his thin chest. "Outside the Mex movie house around the corner. There's a pusher out front. He might do you." The bill disappeared. "Okay, Mac?"

I waved him Godspeed.

The pusher outside the Mex theater was easy to spot because he was a user himself and a lot of his nose had gone in pursuit of the joys of his product. I showed him my calling card downtown, a twenty, double sawbuck. "I'm looking for something that got lost. It was pure and if you had twenty-five million, it would be all yours."

He looked steadily at the bill. "There was something went wrong about two weeks ago. A lotta heat down here."

"Who from?"

He took the bill. "Bastard named Parson."

I shook my head, sighed and tried a tenner this trip. "I said it wrong. I'm looking for a particular product that a big man in the field thought he had."

"Oh," he said. "Shine."

I let him have the bill. "What can you tell me out of pure friendship, pal? I had those names."

He snickered. "Man, are you crazy? Shine's boys been here, there and everywhere. Nobody knows who heisted his package. If they did, they'd be dead. You know Shine."

"I know the man."

"Okay, so whaddaya want? You know who wants it, and you know some smart sonabitch took it. Names I ain't got. That dumb I ain't. But you don't look a nark, so I won't stiff ya.

They're lookin for a broad. Can ya beat that? Some smartass broad beat Shine's time. It's the first dame I heard that crazy."

"You wouldn't know if the product's been milked and is on its way around?"

He looked at me suspiciously. "How come yer innerested?"

"My mother needs a fix."

He sneezed, then grinned. "Send her around. Off the cuff, friend, I ain't hearda nothin movin. Nothin that big. You're talkin a hunnerd pounds pure. We'd all be gettin some of the action and we ain't."

I told him thanks, slipped him another bill and turned.

"Hold it, sport," he said.

"I'm listening."

"This is for free. Lay off. Maybe ya know Shine, like ya say. If ya did, ya wouldn't be askin questions. Go home to yer old lady an' lock the door. This Shine is a shark. Know what I mean? He'll tear ya to pieces."

I shrugged.

"Okay, be a smartass. So I'll tell ya somethin seein ya won't live long enough nohow. The stuff didn't get lost here. Yer a couple hunnerd miles off."

"Frisco?"

"You said it, Jack."

Eighteen

Dill's cryptic message spun a playback in my head. DANTE'S DYNASTY SUNSET SNOWFALL. Checking that one hadn't done any more for me than raising a bump on my noggin. I was fascinated now by the possibility that the tough-sounding Shine could be the Mr. Big I had been hoping to nail all along.

His warehouse, I recalled, was big. So was his threat, his amplified voice, the cocaine shipment gone astray, and undoubtedly his light bill. But if the small-time Venice street pusher knew his name and rep, so would Parson and the other DEA narks up in San Francisco. The underworld figure we had been hunting for was nameless, so far, and very efficient at moving his product. Shine was blaming another for that kind of help.

Parson was my contact man but wouldn't give me the time after our last fracas. I knew I would have to go up there again for the showdown over Dill's snatch and murder, and although I was looking forward to it, it could wait.

I tried Debbie Hill's numbers again but she wasn't home or at the office. I tooled around heading east toward Hollywood and a big red Continental pulled out of a carwash across the street. Pete Tully was behind the wheel.

I had temporarily forgotten the smart-money-type boyfriend of the ex–Mrs. Felix Witter, current night-club chanteuse Kay Morrow. The U-turn my heap went into was good for a ten-dollar rap, but the cruising LAPD black-and-whites were elsewhere. Tully turned and I trailed him down Sunset. He surprised me by wheeling into the lot of Dante's Dynasty.

He walked jauntily into the hair salon, and it's hard these days to know if somebody needs a haircut. While waiting across the street, I hooked into our computer system for a read-out on Shine, the light-bulb king. The index when it came was meager, as if whoever fed the input data didn't want to offend anybody.

Ed (Big Ed) Shine. West Coast syndicate boss, age fifty-two. Jukebox racketeer, gambling boss Oakland area. Cited for heading goon squads in strike breaking against Chavez and farmworkers. Extortion, assault, suspicion of murder. Suspended sentence.

The red car was sitting there and I put Pete Tully's tag through the hopper mix.

Dexter (Pete) Tully. Associated Tony (Big Fish) Canardo, underworld crime boss Los Angeles. Age thirty-six. Employed Las Vegas Starcrest Casino. Dealer, gambler. Five years Folsom State, extortion, assault, attempted bribery and race fixing. Commuted one-to-three.

There was time to kill and ruminate. I checked the mechanical whizzer for current dope on Max Roper. He didn't draw too much.

Government and private security agent West Coast. Age forty-one.

I dialed Dante's. A girl said Mr. Tully couldn't be disturbed for an hour, would I care to leave a message. I said to tell him Ed Shine called from Frisco to send regards.

I drove over to Homicide West on Butler in Camino's bailiwick. He wasn't in and I tried the lower floor and found Doc Shipman at his desk trying to breathe life into another dead cigar.

"You should try the ones that explode," I told him.

He stared up at me. "I know what's eating you. The Witter murder—you're nowhere with the Body Beautiful Caper."

"I'm nowhere with a lot of things. What I'm down here for is a little heart-to-heart talk about this niece of yours."

Shipman shrugged his thin shoulders. "It's up to the girl, Roper. You're okay with me personally, but she's the one who has to decide. Compatibility and all that business."

"The romance hasn't blossomed that far," I said. "Tell me something about her. That is, if you know anything."

"What's to know? She's bright, beautiful, and one hell of a cook, I understand."

I moved my hands. "I was thinking more in genetic terms. Her character, for example. Did she take things from her mommy's purse when she was a little girl? Rifle the old man's pockets, and so forth?"

"If she did," Doc Shipman said, "she was clever enough not to take too much at a clip. What I'm saying is, apparently nobody caught wise. I'm not sure that I understand your question, anyway. Whatever gave you the notion any woman could pass a character test?"

"Skip it," I said. "She told me she'd call to spare you from grieving over her alleged heartbreak over Witter's death. Did she make it?"

My old forensic friend tore the cellophane off a fresh packet of thin stogies. "More or less. But as a grown and gullible man, you ought to know a woman will never admit how she really felt about the last guy in her life."

"She admitted it," I said. "She went through the whole process with me, the living spectrum from love to hate."

Shipman brought flame between his tobacco-stained fingers and puffed up an acrid cloud. "Well, then, there you are. Debbie was clearing the decks for you."

I wigwagged my head. "For me and the world. She's got a thing going with every jock within four hundred miles of here."

"Not too bad a range," Shipman said. "Give her a little time and I'm willing to wager she makes it coast to coast."

"Not the way she's going at it," I said. "The way your niece is doing her life, she may not make it till tomorrow."

Shipman shook his head tolerantly. "Well, now, that's something else. I never figured you for the jealous type. If you can't have her, why kill her? Maybe you can find something closer to your age bracket."

"You're not tuned in on this conversation, Doc. I'm trying to tell you that niece of yours is wanted right now by a big bad guy up Frisco way."

"No problem," Shipman said. "You got all that karate and zip going for you. If you like Deb enough, I'm betting you'll take him."

You get those days where the magic of two-way communication is gone. Baffled, I sought Camino upstairs once more.

"Lieutenant's still out," the desk sergeant said.

"Maybe you can tell me where."

"We got a call some jewel thief ripped up a broad's place. Camino said he had to take care of this personally."

I batted my eyes, looking surprised. "I thought his specialty was homicide."

"Well, yeah," the desk man said, "and Camino said to remind you about that, and you can name the time and place."

The red Continental was gone from Dante's Dynasty lot and I assumed Tully had gone with it. The front door was nail-studded, shaped like a medieval archway, with old worn boards. Inside, it was brighter and more cheerful than on my last visit. The hair-styling stalls lay at opposite sides of the long narrow central aisle. There were bodies in the chairs being attended to by people leaning over them, but the scissors snipped and cut and nobody cried out for help.

There was an opening to the girl at the appointment desk from the anteroom, but to walk through into the working joint required a kind of courage. A black heavy iron portcullis hung high in the rafters, held by thick chains, its sharp rungs menacing overhead. It was the kind of grating or gate that could be hoisted up and down, used to close the gateway of an ancient fortress or castle.

I looked at the blond receptionist from the safer anteroom. She sat with elbows propped over a big appointment book, checking me out, knowing I didn't fit the description she was waiting for.

I thumbed upward to the high dangling relic from the past. "Does that thing work?"

She smiled vacantly. "Gosh, I don't think so. Mr. Dante bought it just for laughs, he said."

"When it comes down on a customer, it should be a good one. Is he in?"

"Mr. Dante? I'll see. Who shall I say is calling?"

"His insurance man. He'll know me."

She pushed herself off the desk and swished down the narrow aisle and disappeared behind a curtained booth. She came out in seconds and hip-swung her way back. She settled carefully into her chair, giving me enough time to check out everything before some of it was put under cover.

"He'll be right with you."

Dante came out walking briskly and I stepped back into the waiting room. He turned the corner and looked at me, and his jaw sagged. He had forgotten that the other man always looks a lot smaller when you've got a hot bird in the sack and can't waste time estimating things.

I made small motions with my hands to make him feel at ease in his own shop. "Forget about the other night," I said. "You had a right to be impatient. Are you working on anybody special right now?"

He grinned. "Only a customer. But, hey, no kidding, I'm sorry I blew my stack. The lieutenant explained to me why you had to be there, your friend getting killed here and so on."

"We're still working on it," I said. "I don't suppose you have anything new to tell me?"

Dante looked sad and concerned. His rotund form swiveled to check the rear booth and make sure his customer wasn't sneaking out the back. "There's nothing I can tell you I didn't tell the lieutenant. Nobody here knows what that was all about."

"Your back door was open when I came in. How did that happen?"

"I dunno. We always lock up. Either I do it myself or Frannie—Miss Corbett does if she's got the last customer." He rubbed his face, sweating. "Frannie . . . you met her that night."

I touched the top of my head. "Yes. Good swing, good solid hit."

"Look, I got to get back. My customers don't like to be all alone in there. Anything else?"

"How long has Pete Tully been a customer here?"

Dante's eyes looked frightened. "Huh? Oh, about a year, I guess. Now, look, I know what you're thinking, but there ain't nothing going on. The man just comes here to have his hair done . . . every three weeks."

"Who's his favorite hair stylist here—you?"

Dante's head said no. "Frannie—Miss Corbett."

"I'd like a few minutes of her time. Okay?"

"Sure. I'll send her right out. And like I said, no hard feelings—okay?"

She came out after a moment, wearing a short white smock, looking nearly as good as she did that night in her brief Baby Doll nightie.

"My name's Roper," I told her. "You wanted to know what I was doing up there that night, remember?"

She bit her luscious lower lip and looked embarrassed. "Hey, look, I'm sorry. I don't even know today where that ashtray came from."

"It happens," I said. "Those things can jump right into a person's hands. But I have a few questions to ask you . . . at your convenience."

She took a step back when I unfurled my wallet with my photo and buzzer. With a passport snap, she might have left her shoes. "Well, like, I'm busy now, y'know . . . a customer. It's all appointments here. You got to move along or he—Mr. Dante don't like it."

"If you're free tonight, and not busy, I can meet you at your apartment, Miss Corbett. It won't take long and you'll have the rest of the night to yourself."

Her hand slapped at her chest. "Okay. Seven-thirty ought to be good. Here. I'll write it down."

114

She took a white card out of her smock pocket and scribbled something on the back. "I put down the phone, too. In case you get hung up."

"No danger. I'll be there. Thanks."

"My pleasure," she said, turning. "See ya later, then."

The hours passed and at the appointed one I was knocking at the door of a small apartment building a few blocks south of the belly-dance joint on Stanley near Sunset. She didn't hear her doorbell any better than my fist on her door.

I waited awhile down in my car and she didn't come along. I got out and found a phone and she wasn't answering that, either. I shook the old worried head and took the heap around to her place of employ and parked in front of Dante's hair salon for men.

The lights were out except for a dim bulb in the rear. I went around the back and the rear door wasn't open this time. I went back to the front and that didn't give, either. I should have called Dante to come over and break open his joint for me, but the hairs on the nape of my neck were bristling and I know the signs for trouble.

My private-eye plastic card slid the front bolt back and I went in. The anteroom was dark and I found the switch on the wall.

She wasn't going to answer any questions tonight or ever because the portcullis had fallen down, its menacing sharp rods skewered into her body, and she lay twisted on the floor, half in and half out of the shop, blood pooling under her trim young body. Her arms were flung out, and her eyes were wide open as if very surprised anybody would want to do such a terrible thing to her.

Nineteen

There was time to look over the appointment book from the anteroom opening before Camino came down. It would have been more fun with Frannie Corbett wearing something comfortable, short and gauzy, telling me that indeed she had been trimming the golden locks of the body-building champ Felix Witter. But the notations in the book told me as much without the body-stress involvement, and probably had a better memory, putting Felix down for his bimonthly appointments at his regular time of 6 P.M.

It took an earlier book under the counter ledge to convince me that Witter was an older and more loyal customer than Pete Tully, although his appointment times varied, sometimes being marked for the noon hour.

Tully was a Johnny-come-lately comparatively, his personal hair styling beginning a shade less than six months previous. His appointment time was erratic, varying between late morning and late afternoon.

Miss Frannie Corbett was the designated hitter with the shears and clippers for both men. There were five other hair-pulling experts for the shop, including Firpo Dante himself, and none of them worked over any name I knew.

There wasn't anything about this I wanted to discuss with my homicidal friend Camino, and I wasn't in the mood to hear his forensic pathologist Doc Shipman explaining to me how Frannie lost the ball game in the gluteal region at a point between the serratus posterior inferior and the gluteus maximus, perforating that part of the dorsum ilii which is bounded above by the posterior curved line and the anterior crest of the ilium, the internal pudendal artery, the pudendal nerve and the nerve and obdurator internus muscle, severing laterally the sacrospinous ligaments and attachments to the spine.

Luckily I had committed Cunningham's *Manual of Practical Anatomy* to memory and knew all of Volume One from Superior Extremity to Inferior Extremity.

It was eight o'clock—a good time to hit somebody, but I didn't know where to start. I got back into my heap and waited till I saw the flashing redtops of Camino's finest, and was around the corner before the wailing sirens wound down.

Santa Monica was next, along Wilshire. The restaurant was owned at one time by a famous night-club comic but had passed on to newer hands. The food wasn't bad, and the hat-check girl filled out her black mesh stockings, but this time I was more interested in the bouncer.

His name was Steve Shaw and he had been a Mr. America and Mr. Olympia, and maybe if he hadn't thrown his wife out the window for one of the things wives sometimes do when motels aren't handy, he might have gone on to be Mr. Universe, Mr. World and whatever.

He had put on a little weight after a brief time in the pokey but could still take a punch from a drunk customer, smile politely and then deck him with either hand.

"You look like you're working out again," I said.

His right hand shot out and gripped my shoulder without cracking the bone. "Hey, am I glad to see you! Where ya been?"

I tried shrugging with the off shoulder. "Around. Busy."

"Wise guy, I never got a chance to thank you."

I looked around. "It doesn't look that much of a job. How many do you have to punch out a night?"

Steve grinned. "It varies. Sometimes they don't believe it and come back with a friend. I get a couple two-on-one heats that keep me in shape."

"So what can you tell me about Felix Witter?"

"Oh, business, huh?"

"How well did you know him, if at all?"

"Oh, hell, I knew Felix. Used to work out with him when he was first getting started, down at the old Fifth Street gym."

"How long ago?"

"Five, ten years. Let's see, Johnny Albany was the big man then, just came off his Mr. A win—yeah, so it was ten, I guess. Johnny was closer to him than me, started giving Felix tips—like, his secrets, y'know. He just took a shine to the kid. But, like, whattaya wanna know?"

"Everybody I talk to hated his guts. Why?"

The big bouncer shrugged massive arms and shoulders that seemed to cover the sidewalk. "I dunno. Felix wasn't too polite, I guess. He just did what he wanted, took what he wanted."

"Women, too?"

"What else we talking about?"

"Anybody in particular?"

"Nobody I remember. That type—they're all pretty much the same, y'know. Go for the body. Gotta have it any way they can." He sighed. "They want the Greek gods with the figleaf off."

"Was Witter yellow?"

Shaw looked at me surprised. "Is that a real question?"

I nodded.

He scratched the back of his head. "About what? The guy was so big, even then, who'd wanna mess with him to find out?"

"Maybe somebody who didn't want Witter cutting in on his own action with some broad."

"Oh, like that? Well, I dunno. If I remember, he took Albany's girl. Maybe he was bigger, but still, Johnny boy was the champ. Felix didn't think twice, he just moved in."

"You wouldn't remember her name?"

Shaw shook his curly head. "Nah, too long ago. I think maybe Kay something . . . I forget. She was some kind of cute stacked

118

blonde, like a lotta them were." He grinned. "Maybe I oughtta say, still are."

"How about yourself? Did Witter take anything of yours?"

Shaw's strong white teeth flashed in a wide grin. "You kidding? I'da killed him." He frowned. "Well, you know me—the old hot-temper kid. But no, he never rubbed me the wrong way. I even kinda liked the guy. It's the other kind I never liked, the guys always smiling at'cha—the con guys."

"Give me one for a starter, Steve."

"Well, take Johnny A. I guess Albany's the biggest con guy we ever had in our racket. Made it big, too, all the way. So it figures, maybe you gotta be that way."

"What way?"

"You know. You keep smiling when you wanna deck some smart apple. You shake his mitt and wish him lotsa luck, all that crapola. Then, when you're ready, you make your move, you got the guy suckered out, he thinks you're his buddy. He's got ya by the balls alla time, only ya don't know it."

"Did Johnny Albany sucker Witter that way?"

"Well, that I dunno. I been away the last couple years, y'know. I hear Witter was doin stuff for him, promotin his product, but I dunno what kinda deal Felix had. So I dunno who was suckering who. Back five, ten years, Johnny was no business freaking success yet, remember. Just the best body builder around."

"Any idea who might have killed Felix?"

My body-building buddy shook his head from side to side. "Nah, that was too crazy to figure. Sure, maybe Felix was some kinda pain inna ass to a lotta people, but so what? I mean, who ain't? To kill a guy like that, all the years sweating out the iron, pulling the hunnerd, two hunnerd tons a day, four, five hours a day, six, seven days a week, ten years working your ass off, busting your balls, killing yourself inside alla time, hurting, torturing the body for more, living with the pain night and day, and then to have some freak knock you off after you made best inna world—man, that gets me mad!"

My stocky friend was getting charged up, looking wild-eyed,

119

and I was glad I wasn't the man he had found messing with his sweet-talking Susan, the wife who broke his heart and brought him to murder. I stepped back, lit a butt and let him wind down. "Do you know how Witter was killed?"

Shaw grimaced. "What's the difference? Poisoned, I heard. Somebody slipped a goofball into one of his high-protein pills? Or maybe his vitamin bottle?"

I shook my head, and explained how it was done. Shaw stared at me, his thick black eyebrows raised, mouth open, looking as shocked as the kid who found out Santa Claus worked for the May Company.

"Jesus, Roper—ya gotta be kidding!"

"No. Somebody who wanted Witter dead switched rubbing-oil bottles on him."

"Jesus, whatta freaking thing to do!"

"Not too tough a trick. Remember when you were in competition? How often would you check what you had in your oil bottle?"

He shrugged. "Jesus—like, never! It lasts, y'know, like, forever. Ya run short, ya borrow some from the guy next to you. Then, when ya get home, if ya remember, ya put some more of the gook in. Otherwise ya forget, and ya borrow again. What the hell, everybody uses the same stuff to oil up. I mean, it ain't no magic secret formula. It's just the same crappy oil."

I didn't like this new information because it suggested somebody else could have been the target, and Witter's death an accident. Even without Shine to worry about, I'd never live long enough to check out all the body builders in that sweaty backstage room, nor the tendrils of their backgrounds that might account for that kind of deliberate murder.

I got off oil and back into character assassination. "What do you know about Eddie Blue?"

"Eddie? He's okay. Kind of a wheeler-dealer like Johnny A. I think he's a good pick for second with Witter around. With Felix dead, Eddie's gotta be number one. He works hard, real hard."

"Now a few women, Steve—did you ever know a Mrs. Marilyn Channing?"

120

Steve grinned and shook his hand as if it suddenly became too hot. "Oh yeah, I seen her a lot. Felix brought her here a lot. Some dish! Also I seen her with Johnny Albany, and also Eddie Blue."

"How about with her husband?"

"I wouldn't know the sucker."

"Just one more—a girl by the name of Debbie Hill."

Somehow the name brought up the simmering violence of my thickset buddy. "Hey, come on! Whaddaya doing? Lay off, will ya? I know Deb—she's a hunnerd-percent nice kid."

"Nothing personal, Steve. I heard she was Felix Witter's girl, too."

Shaw looked sullen, sounded surlier. "Jesus, that's a crock! I dunno whatcha mean, 'his girl'! If they went out a couple times, that make her his girl? Jesus, come on now, I'm tellin ya, Deb's a real nice kid."

I grinned. "You sound like you like her a little yourself."

He flushed like a schoolboy. "Well, yeah—I mean, I know I'm too old and like that, but I seen her at the health talk shows, y'know? I really dig the way Deb moves and how she talks. And she's built, too, real good. She don't know I'm alive, but I really like that lady."

"Maybe you ought to keep looking. I understand she has a thing going with Eddie Blue now."

Shaw scowled. "Aw, come on, that's bullshit! If there's one guy I know for sure Deb don't go for, it's Eddie B."

"What makes you so sure?"

"None of your freaking business, buddy."

"This is still an investigation, Steve. Nothing personal."

"Okay. Eddie brought her down here one time. On the way out, he tried to grab her in the parking lot. She hadda deck him right over his car."

I stared. "Debbie Hill did that to Eddie Blue?"

Steve smiled. "Well, I gave her a little help." He caught my suspicious stare and shrugged. "Well, what the hell, it's my job here, ain't it? I'm the bouncer you told them to hire to stop people from messing or getting messed."

Twenty

This time when the chunky roly-poly hairdresser Dante answered his door, I wasn't about to get suckered. I cold-decked him at sight with a stiff left, closed the door behind me and waited for him to get up. There wasn't any soft music playing, no twittery bird in the boudoir waiting to zap me with a piece of crockery, and I was feeling mean and ugly and impatient.

He sat up on his expensive carpet piling, rubbing his jaw and looking up at me as if I'd wronged him somehow. "Now, hey, look, friend—what's that all about?"

"A couple of hours ago I found your little friend Frannie all alone in your shop. Somehow somebody had dropped your cute portcullis on her so that she was very dead. You take it from there, friend."

He looked genuinely shocked, but then, I meet a lot of good actors in the line. "You got to be kidding," he said hoarsely, big dark eyes rolling. "Frannie dead . . . that way?" I nodded sternly and he added, "Omigod!"

"Why did you buy that doohicky, anyway?" I said.

Dante shrugged. "I dunno . . . the designer-architect sold me a bill of goods. Atmosphere, he called it. Like the door outside. I thought maybe it was cute—different, anyway—and bought it."

"What's his name?"

"Tracy. Keith Tracy. But now, look . . . he's gay . . . I don't think—"

122

"Don't think. Get up and sit in a chair. We've got a lot of talking tonight between us."

He shoved himself up, wobbled toward his black leather Miller chair. "Take it easy, man. I'm straight, I tell you. I got nothing to hide."

"Let's finish with the mystery of the falling gateway first. How often has it been dropped?"

He massaged his throat. "This way like tonight? Jesus—never! When I first opened the place, Tracy told me how it worked. You just release the chains hooked on top and ease it down. The idea was, the customer comes in and when the broad gives him the high sign says he's okay, the shine boy lifts it up. He hooks it again on top on each side, the john goes through.

"But we did it only a couple times the first day and it got to be a pain in the ass. Nobody trusted us about coming through under it, and got nervous again coming out. So I'm not dumb, I figured screw it, the hell with that jazz. I had it tied up good and tight on the hooks on top, and decided to just keep it as a decoration, like for laughs. That's it, I swear. Nobody ever played any games with that mother."

"What time did you leave your shop tonight?"

"My last customer was five to six. I left right after, maybe six-fifteen. I get in early, around eight. That's a long enough day for me. I'm not fixing to get rich."

"How many of your staff were left working then?"

"Only two. Number three booth, Clyde Bush—he had his boyfriend to finish. He'd be done at six-thirty. Then Frannie down at the end, her spot booth six. She had a six o'clock john, but he still hadn't shown for his appointment. She said she'd wait around, give him till six-thirty to come or call in, and then she'd close up. She's done that a lot, Frannie. Good kid, been with me for years."

"What was Frannie's john's name?"

"Medwick. Joey Medwick. He's one of the boys, a friend of Pete Tully, so naturally we give him a little break and don't close the door in his face, he's a little late."

"He's been late before?"

Dante shrugged. "Hell, everybody's been late. Being late for your hairdresser appointment don't scare too many people."

"How about Felix Witter? Did he screw up his appointments too, when he felt like it?"

"Now, that's a funny thing," Dante said. "Of all my regular customers, I think Witter maybe was the only guy who was always on time, who never stiffed us with some far-out excuse. Big as the guy was—you know what he looked like, like he could knock the place down—Witter was real low-key with us, a nice, sweet regular guy."

"Miss Corbett was always his stylist?"

"Well, yeah. Matter of fact, that's how they come together. Frannie came to me from another place. She brought her own customers along, like they do. Witter was one."

I had the notebook ready again. "What place and how long ago, Mr. Dante?"

"The place was Galahad, run by Alan Baker. He was about the first of the men's stylists out here. When? About five years back. I picked up a lotta people in that time. You lose a few, you get some new ones."

"How do you pick your hair stylists?"

Dante shrugged. "It's a business. Anybody can do the hair. You want somebody who's got a list. You rent out space to them, they gotta produce. I need one good day a week to take care of the nut—the rent."

"Did Frannie date her customers?"

"It was up to her, it's her life. When she had nothing better to do, she'd come up here for some laughs."

"Was she your steady girl? I mean, off-hours."

He shook his head. "No, you got that wrong, Roper. I can get all I want. We got two other kids there as good as Fran in the sack any time. If they're too busy, I got friends all around. Maybe you don't know it, women dig hairdressers. Maybe it's like a quest, to find out if we got balls for them."

"Maybe," I said. "Last time around now. Can you think of anybody who wanted Miss Corbett dead?"

Headshake. "No. Especially not . . . that way. Jesus!"

"Frannie take care of Pete Tully, too?"

"Yeah. But she didn't bring him in like Witter. He came in one time, asked for the best, I gave him Frannie."

"Any of the other weight men come in here? Johnny Albany, for instance? Eddie Blue?"

"No sir. I don't know those names. Mr. Witter was the only one we had like that."

"Where's your phone?"

He blinked. "There's one in the kitchen."

I watched him and saw he didn't have any plans, and stepped into the kitchen. It was a wall-clasp connection and I ripped it all off and came back to Dante.

"Where's the other one?"

"Bedroom."

"Stay put. I'm in a terrible mood tonight."

I brought the bedroom phone back on its long white cord. Dante watched apprehensively as I dialed and asked for Homicide. The deskman gave me the old story. Camino wasn't in, he was out on a body hunt. I gave the sergeant the names Dante had thrown in, told him I would be back at my pad later if Camino was interested.

"Nick called back right away on this one, Roper," the man said. "He wanted you to stay put tonight to explain a few things."

"He knows where I live, Dave," I said and ripped the cord out.

Dante sulked. "I use those phones for business, too, you know."

I threw a twenty down on the table. "Tomorrow you can call up for repairs. I didn't want any of those people getting uptight and leaving town before they were asked some questions."

Dante didn't throw me a kiss when I left, but looked happier when he saw I meant it. It was close to ten o'clock when I got back to my joint. I parked the heap out front on the street so I wouldn't be sandbagged, went into the hall of the next apartment braced to mine, up to the top two stories and over the roof and down to mine. I didn't meet anybody on the way and I didn't feel like getting killed for a few hours.

The phone was ringing when I got the door open. I took it on the run and heard a voice I thought I was beginning to dislike.

"Where have you been?" she said. "I've been calling you for hours."

"First things first, Miss Hill. Where are you calling from?"

"San Francisco."

"Feed me the number, please."

She did that. "Now, what I wanted to say—"

"Is that a private home, apartment or hotel, Miss Hill?"

"An apartment, but—"

"I'll take the address and apartment number, please." She gave me that reluctantly, I thought, and I asked whose name was listed down in the mail slot. She didn't want to answer that one. "You called and I know you're in trouble," I said. "Better give it to me." She told me then—Mundy.

"If you're coming up, I'll wait," she offered.

"Good idea. That's a very rough neighborhood you're nesting in. Lock your door, and if there's somebody with you, get rid of him. I'll hop the next flight up."

I hung up fast and went out, up, over and down the same way I'd come in. Traffic was light and I made good time and got hold of the Proud Bird's tail before it could go off without me.

The flight gave me an hour to sort things out. It was midnight on the nose when we touched in. A cab took me to Chinatown and I got off on Grant a few blocks before Sproule Lane to check the neighborhood.

The tourist shops were closed, the restaurants open, people walking the street. The number she had given me was one of a series of old apartment buildings off a narrow and crooked dark alley. A few lights glowed upstairs. Cars were parked across the street with nothing more suspicious than hard guys inside. Men lounged against the alley walls, hands in their pockets, watching the sucker move in.

I lit a match in the dark hallway and buzzed Mundy. The

outer door opened and I went through without being busted. The stairs were old and musty, the cooking smells terrific. Egg foo yong and pork spareribs were on the menu. The house smelled like a hideout for a renegade Chinese chef.

I toiled up three flights. Outside the door, I listened long enough and knocked. The door opened with my hand on the knob. I stepped in and saw her briefly across the room, looking beautiful and twice as scared. I was thinking about that when the door closed behind me and something no harder or heavier than a building fell on my head. As I was going down to birdie land, the only one I could think of willing and able to hit me that hard would be the big DEA ape, Parson.

My eyes flicked open and saw him standing there grinning before I blacked out.

Twenty-one

Nobody writes the song about how it is in San Francisco when you're alone in a room with a pretty girl and a nasty big hard man, and while the man keeps knocking you down and hauling you up so he can knock you off your feet again, the girl sits there mute, only her eyes registering emotion, as if she's judging the contest and giving the other guy all the points.

Parson was making good on all the rotten things my friend Camino said about him. He didn't go by rules and never heard of sportsmanship and fair play, and concentrated instead on getting all the hate out of his system by knocking me all over the room, breaking me up inside, messing me a lot on the outside, and generally demonstrating that it's not that hard to destroy a karate man if you get the first good blow in and scramble his brains.

After a good thudding over, I forgot my name along with my karate. The big thing I had to learn this night was push-ups off the floor and I was getting better at it. My nose felt spread from ear to ear and I was choking on my own blood. But that didn't bother Parson, who was still strong, unmarked, having one of the better times of his life.

I had long since lost count of my trips to the carpet and was on my hands and knees trying to get up, very tired and not sure I could make it. Parson came over and saved me the trouble by kicking my right rib cage in and I rolled over. He had his leg up ready for the next stomping shot and my weary old brain said "*Enough* already!"

I lashed out with ankle kick *(kansetsu-geri)*, catching his knee at the side, and the target leg he was balancing on buckled. I twisted and gave him heel kick *(kakato-geri)*, letting his standing ankle get the full impact of my down-thrust stamping foot. Parson cursed and wobbled and came lower and when he was close enough, I gave him groin kick, my knee as the fulcrum, Parson's scream my supreme joy.

I got up now happier with my own martial music blaring away inside and found him with the knee kick as he came charging in. Leg thrusts are more powerful than arm moves, and my knee whooshed deep into his gut and Parson's eyes spun.

It was more fun for the good guys now, and I gave him all the nice moves, like rising elbow strike, which is an elbow uppercut at your opponent's chin. It didn't tear Parson's head off but he sagged again, and I caught him coming down with the descending elbow strike.

It was all my ballgame now and I gave him driving knife-hand strike to the collar bone and heard it snap, then knife-hand strike to the face, breaking the bastard's nose and spattering him with his own blood.

He backed up a step, snuffling, one arm dangling low. He wiped the blood off his face with the back of his hand and it didn't make him any happier. I didn't want to give him too much breathing time, but I needed some answers. "What happened with Dill, Parson? Who wasted him?"

He showed me a horrible twisted grin and a few missing teeth. "Dill couldn't wait," he said thickly, his throat clogged with his blood. "He was a smartass like you. Thought he had all the answers and could move in." He chuckled. "He thought he could beat my time. Nobody does that."

"I hear you don't like that. Did you kill him?"

He snickered. "I didn't have to. Somebody beat me to it."

"I heard a pistol shot when you were on the phone with me."

Parson wagged his head, his chest heaving, sucking air.

"Don't believe everything you hear, sucker. I got my own ways to play games, y'know."

I didn't want Parson to take all the air in the room and sucked up some myself, wondering if I looked as bad to him as he did to me. "What about Miss Hill? What's your game with her, you dumb ape?"

Parson thought about it and decided he didn't like what I said. "You'll never know, sucker, because I'm taking you out right now."

He came at me, flailing with his good right arm. I side-stepped and gave him inverted-fist low thrust deep into his solar plexus, making him grunt.

I never would have thought of throwing Parson through the window, but those things happen when everybody gets charged up. He came at me again like a wounded bull, swinging his thick powerful arm, looking like another monster that got away from Dr. Frankenstein. I stepped aside, and as he went by, gave him forefist roundhouse strike. Parson, who was very fast for a big man, stumbled, tottered, threw his arms up and crashed through the glass. He yelled something blood-curdling on the way down.

Stepping back, a bloodied and battered wreck, I glanced over toward where I had seen the girl last. She was looking at her wristwatch, a frown on her face, making me wish I hadn't kept her from an important date. I shrugged at the smashed window and the yawning darkness. "So much for that. With luck, he landed on his head and may still be alive."

Miss Hill said, "Would you mind untying me, please?"

True blue, I said to myself, and she definitely would have leaped to my rescue bashing Parson with any number of the handy things girls can improvise into instant weapons, but with hands tied thusly, ankles taped to the chair, truly she could do nothing.

I unknotted the thongs about her wrists and took a bit more time on the adhesives over the ankles. She did have marvelous legs, and removing tape can be a painful process. It's always best to go slowly, patting the circulation back into play as you move along.

130

Miss Hill forgot her place in the feminist charter for a few seconds, then said, "Would you mind turning your head just a bit? You're bleeding on my skirt."

I made short shrift of the remaining tape. "My going rates for rescues are a trifle higher in Chinatown. If you're a little short on ready cash, I'm willing to wait until we get a sale on that twenty-five-million-dollar snow heist. I'll settle for twenty percent, my finder's fee, and you can have the twenty-odd million left."

She rubbed her legs herself and it didn't look that much better a job. "What on earth are you talking about?"

I stood up and stared down, not too difficult really when you get it all together. "The heist on Mr. Shine's cocaine. Didn't you know you're a much-wanted fugitive from a couple of ugly-looking hitmen?"

She looked at me puzzled. "I know you've taken a bad beating about the head, but—"

I leveled my forefinger in her direction. "Why do you think Parson tied you up here and got you to sucker me down?"

"I really don't know. He's been following me for some time. I thought it was—well, something else he wanted."

"He's a lot bigger than you—or was. Why would he have to tie you up, Miss Hill?"

"For excitement, I thought. You know these lurid pictures you see on all the suspense paperbacks."

I held out my hand. "Come on, maybe you'll remember where you stashed the stuff on the way. I hear sirens coming."

She got up and went along peaceably for a few steps. "Just a moment, please. I think you'd better tell me what this is all about. I honestly don't understand a word you're saying."

I heard noises downstairs from the street and knew there wasn't too much time to explain things to a stubborn woman. "First of all, Parson, the man who went out the window, is . . . was a DEA man."

"What's that?"

"A state nark—Drug Enforcement Administration. His job has to do with the illegal import of narcotic goods—that would be like drugs, hard drugs. And somehow he found out, like myself and a lot of much meaner and unforgiving people, that somewhere along the line you managed to swipe a load of stardust, commonly known as cocaine, destined for a big mobster in this area called Shine.

"Shine had his boys pull me in and told me to get the vitamin broad, which I had to assume was you, and get back his twenty-five-million-buck shipment, or else! The 'or else' includes your own sweet self, Miss Hill. All clear now?"

She stamped her foot with the best. "Are you crazy? What would I be doing stealing that—did you say snowdust?"

"I don't know why. Usually it's for money, because this stuff is pure, and the twenty-five million will sell in time for ten times that much. I imagine you thought you had it made when you told me you hadn't seen Felix Witter in two months. It was more recently—say, two weeks—wasn't it?"

She looked about as contrite as I could ever hope her to be, and it wasn't too much. "Well, there was no way to explain that to a man so that he would understand. I was finished with Felix, as I told you. But he called me a few weeks ago and asked if I could do him a small favor, that it was terribly important and had nothing to do with renewing our relationship. On that basis, I agreed."

I waved my hands. "Okay, enough for now. You'll fill me in on the way down there. You may have some explaining to do later to a lot of government people, if we can manage to keep it from Shine. But I'll take your word for it for now, and we'll pick it up again later. Okay?"

She hesitated, the dark-blue eyes smoldering, but then she tossed her head, shrugged and said, "I'm agreeing for now because I find this conversation very boring."

I nodded and reached for the door. "Believe me, boring is the last thing this caper is. For example, right now—"

The door opened, and the example was there before our very eyes. Two men stood in the doorway. One had a sawed-off shotgun, the other had a big .38 and a nervous grip on it.

"As I was saying," I told her, "these are a few of the parties concerned who work for the bigger party. That one is Lew. This one is Charley. They do funny things, but take my word for it—the guns are real."

Twenty-two

"Jesus, ya look terrible," Charley said, "but thanks for Parson, that was a good hit."

"Yeah," Lew said. "That sonofabitch was a real pain in the ass!" He caught himself, pulled the piece an inch away from Miss Hill and said, "Excuse me, lady."

I scuttled inside the car close behind Miss Hill to rid Charley of his head-rapping habit. He shrugged off his disappointment and I settled back in the rear seat waiting for him to join us. "Where we going?" I said.

Charley got in. "Maybe you can make a good guess. Move it, Lew."

"I can't," Lew said.

"Why the hell not?" Charley demanded.

"Look for yourself."

"Where the hell I look, jerk?"

"Straight ahead."

Charley peered through the glass straight ahead. "Oh yeah—roadblock."

Miss Hill tossed her head and hair. "I think this is all ridiculous. I'm leaving."

Charley prodded my side with his gun. "Hey, is she kidding?"

"I don't think she understands the situation, Charley."

He waved the gun under my nose. "Maybe you explain it, huh?"

134

"It's only a short ride, Miss Hill," I told her. "We would all appreciate your company."

She looked at me coldly, the big rescue scene behind her, unimpressed, illogical, as some of them are. "Well, I hope you know what you're doing." She glanced at her watch. "I've a lecture to give back in Los Angeles before noon."

"Plenty of time," I said. "Barring Mr. Shine's being unreasonable, we'll make it easy."

A siren wailed from behind.

"Jesus," Lew said, "now they got one behind us."

"Maybe we better walk," Charley said. "It's this jerk Roper's fault. If he didn't chuck the guy outta the window, we'd be there already."

"I'm real sorry," I said. "Parson was killing me."

Charley nodded slowly, frowning. "Yeah, but it don't help now. C'mon, let's ditch the car and—"

"I'm too beat to walk, Charley," I said. "Why don't you cut through the alley here? There's Jackson on the other side, and you can cut through Montgomery or Kearny down to the water."

"Hey, that's a thought," Charley said. "You hear that, Lew?"

"I ain't deaf," Lew said. He backed the car up a half length and turned into the alley. "Looks clear up ahead. Whattaya think, Charley, okay?"

Charley chewed on his lip. "Looks okay." He turned to me. "What if they got one there, too, pal?"

"I don't see anything. Maybe they don't know the alley runs through." I shrugged. "It's worth a shot. Here you're dead."

"Okay, Lew," Charley said. "We stay here, we're dead. It's worth a shot."

The car moved forward slowly. The alley was narrow and occasionally a rubbish tin disputed our progress. Lew moved relentlessly onward over and around the clattering cans.

"Jesus," Lew said. "Why the hell don't they clean up this place?"

There weren't any patrols as we nosed into the street ahead.

135

Lew nodded gratefully and swung right. "Worked okay. Thanks, Roper, I gotta remember that shortcut."

I felt Miss Hill tensing on my left. "Why are you helping these men?" she whispered into my near ear.

I shrugged. "We have to clear up this mystery, Miss Hill. When you tell Mr. Shine where the stuff is, all will be well."

She shook her head. "I haven't been to sleep yet but I know this is all a bad dream."

"It all goes back to the favor you agreed to do for Felix Witter, for old times' sake. My guess is that it included picking up a small package, perhaps a few small ones. True or false?"

"You're insane! That was for Freddie Guest."

"Before or after he was dead?"

"Before, obviously," she snapped. "Or do you think I killed Freddie and then ran and stashed his package of snowdust?"

"It's possible," I said. "Maybe you, Guest and Dr. Holt have been engaged in interesting and profitable sidelines." I rubbed my swollen jaw and turned on Charley. "Shine gave me five days. How come you cut my time tonight?"

Charley shook his head. "Ya got it wrong, pal. You just happened along. We wasn't going for you. It was her—the dame. We had her tagged, and when the nark Parson picked her up, we stayed close. Shine decided we don't wait no more after midnight."

"Midnight? You mean, if I wasn't there, you would have knocked off Parson?"

"Well, sure. Like I said, we had orders."

"Maybe you guys better learn how to tell time. At midnight I was there waltzing around with the man. Where were you?"

Charley frowned. "We had a accident." He addressed the driver. "Right, Lew? We call it a accident?"

The driver Lew bobbed his head. "Don't laugh, Roper, but while we was watchin the house for Parson and the twist, some rotten lousy little kid let the air outta the front tire. I had to go get the flat fixed and let Charley take over the stake by hisself. Them kids today, they're all rotten wiseguys. They got no respeck for nothin."

I turned back to the feminist filly and vitamin broad. "How's the old memory? Getting any flashes of recall? Your friend Freddie Guest had an awful lot of money stashed away in a coffee can. Was that the small favor Witter wanted? I hear he had a great fondness for money."

She shrugged it off. "What time do you think we'll be finished with all this nonsense?"

"Charley," I said, "what's your guess?"

"Jeez, I dunno—it all depends. The boss is mad." He addressed the driver. "Right, Lew? He's mad?"

Lew answered over his shoulder. "He's mad."

Charley ticked them off on his left hand with his gun. "So that's point one, Shine's mad. Point two is the dame. Does she come up with the stuff, or maybe she already unloaded? Point three, maybe it's been cut and so Shine gets now maybe four parts quinine. Which brings us back to point one—Shine's mad. So, it all depends."

"There's your answer, Miss Hill," I said. "It all depends."

"I think you're all crazy," she said. "If you don't mind, I prefer not to discuss any of this, until we get to where we're supposed to be going."

"Right up ahead," Charley said.

I smelled the waterfront and fish. The driver went past Bimbo's on Columbus heading for Fisherman's Wharf. He turned left at North Point, then right again, and we were on Jefferson with the fish shanties and grottoes, the canning companies, fish smokehouses. The Dolphin Club is near there, and the South End Rowing Club, the ropemakers and boat repair shops. There was a narrow opening this side of the Hyde Park pier and Lew slid in there. I could see the old sailing ships in the water, the lights bobbing, and the fogged dim outline of the big warehouse just off the Bay.

Apart from Shine and me having business together, my hope was he would put a little realistic fear into the heart of the recalcitrant vitamin broad. Fear is very good for jogging the memory, putting all those tired, snotty memory cells back on the track. She fielded my questions too easily and I wanted Shine for my designated hitter.

Lew stopped the car smoothly. He got out and stood there ready to have a shot at the health-addict girl in the event she found some early foot. Charley went out on his side, tapping me gently with the .38. "Let's go, sport."

I touched Miss Hill's arm. It was warm, firm and surprisingly electric. All those atomic vitamins in there. "Remember your uncle Shipman loves you, and will miss you," I told her. "You're out of his area and he won't be able to do his forensic stuff over your bloated body, to find out how long you were in the water inside all that hard, heavy cement. So be a good girl and don't try to screw around with Mr. Shine. Don't ask who did his lighting. Just tell the truth and maybe we'll all live."

She bared her teeth but didn't bite. "I think that other man really punched your brains out."

She stepped out, legs flashing, without my offering a hand. Charley's eyes caught mine. They locked and his flicked. He was telling me this was the last stop and I knew he knew I knew. Or perhaps Miss Hill had correctly estimated the postcranial damage in the Parson affair.

We all went into Shine's warehouse hoping for the best.

Twenty-three

The scene was the same old spooky cavernous warehouse, but Shine had cut down on his light bill and was trying for his master's in dramatic effects. The interior was dark and relieved only by patches of pale moonlight filtering through the high windows on the concrete floor. Our hollow-sounding footsteps sent an echoing clatter high up in the rafters. The big wooden crates stood in dark shadowy pools, and a birthday candle would have made it big this night.

A light glowed dimly at the far end. We walked closer and saw that it was a light behind a glass partition. The partition became an office door. We stopped short and Charley tapped it politely. It seemed a ridiculous touch after sounding off over a hundred feet of solid staccato echoes but it worked.

The door opened and immediately I preferred the old Shine, the hazy light-splintered distorted outline impossible to see clearly. He wasn't any bigger than the entire right side of the Ram line, and he couldn't have been uglier than Yeti the Abominable Snowman from the Himalayas. With such a gross employer behind the take-home pay and fringe benefits or otherwise, I could now better understand the continuing anxiety state of Lew and Charley.

"Roper wasted Parson," Charley said quickly, "so we brung him along with the dame. Okay?"

Shine nodded, saving his dialogue for a better moment. He looked to be in his mid-fifties, his face roughly carved out of splintered granite, resembling my idea of Neanderthal man's older and meaner brother, the one who tortured his pet saber-toothed tiger and kicked the mammoth out of his playpen.

He thumbed his two soldiers out and closed the door. He balefully looked down at Miss Hill without buckling her knees and went behind his desk and sat down. He spread his big hands apart and tapped out a minor melody on the desktop with his gnarled broken fingers. They were thick and had knitted together badly, but Shine didn't need them to punch me out because between his hands was a big black Colt .45 automatic.

Miss Hill couldn't wait for bad news to happen. She took a step forward, leaving me alone against the wall, and addressed Mr. Ed (Big Ed) Shine in ringing tones remindful of her last lecture to the Bay Area Friends of Organic Foods. "May I ask what this ridiculous charade is all about?"

Shine's large gray eyes rolled to mine and I gave him number-one shrug for "Beats the hell outta me, Jack." He sighed, lifted his huge chest in a deep breath and blew out his cheeks, shaking his head, sadly but positively. "You wanna know," he said. "That's rich. But just so there's no mistake, I'll tell you. Then you know and I don't say it two times. Okay? You got my product, I dunno how, but you got it. Now either I get it back, lady, or you're very dead."

In my eagerness for Miss Hill to meet up face to face with a genuinely mean underworld character like Shine, I had forgotten she knew so many outsize jocks that she was quite used to big ugly men, perhaps adjusted to being fond of them at first sight. Instead of quailing before Shine's threatening bulk, she smiled and lifted her forefinger in an admonishing gesture. "I'm afraid, Mr. Shine, that you are laboring under the same delusion as Mr. Parson was, and also Mr. Roper here. I have nothing of yours, no product, to the best of my knowledge. And you've cost me a night's sleep, which will make it very difficult for me to do a good job on my lecture later this morning."

Shine listened without blinking. He glanced at me again, but I

140

had already given him my best pantomime bit of no-knowledge and waited passively. "You was seen," Shine said. "Now, lady, don't gimme no hard time. You was *seen.*

"Two weeks ago a truck pulls up here at night with my stuff in it. I got two men on it, and both dumb assholes get out to put the tailgate down. Only some guy steps up outta left field and puts the crunch on my two boys. One croaks but the other lives long enough to fill me in.

"He says the big heister was Witter, the muscle you travel with. He says the broad waiting in the car was you, the vitamin broad. Then he, too, dies—but remember, he already seen you.

"Why d'ya think Parson was workin you over? He's a state nark, see, only he works for me, he's on the take. Parson tells me the same thing, it's you and Witter. Only he's dead now, which leaves only you. Okay, you got it?"

Miss Hill stamped her foot impatiently. "I'm sorry, but somehow you have your facts wrong, Mr. Shine. It's true that I did see Felix two weeks ago, but it wasn't anywhere near here and it wasn't at night. I saw him one morning, I don't remember exactly when, but it was the first and last time I'd seen him in at least two months."

Shine shrugged, his voice dull but sounding a growling note. "Okay, so now it ain't night, it's morning. So he gave you the stuff to stash, right? Now be a good girl, lady, or else—"

Miss Hill shook her lovely obstinate head. "He did nothing of the kind. Now will you be good enough and let me out of here or do I have to call the police?"

Shine blew his cheeks out again and got up. "Jesus, what a bigmouth," he said.

"Mr. Shine," I said. "I don't think Miss Hill understands—"

"She'll get it," he said. "Only I'll just hafta slap it outta her, is all."

"I don't get it about Parson," I said quickly. "Charley told me he had orders to kill Parson tonight after midnight. How does that check with Parson working for you?"

Shine grinned. "Parson's no dope. He figures he's got the dame, he'll get the dope. Maybe later he'll do me a big favor and sell it back to me for a little profit. Maybe he'll double-cross me. So I'm wise to the bastard and I give my boys the orders. They get the broad, who needs him? He was trouble, anyway. Sooner or later, he got to go."

He lifted his hand and slapped Miss Hill across her left cheek. "You talk, sister, or I kill you inch by inch. Where's my stuff?"

Miss Hill rattled against Shine's office wall, taking the blow well and showing no signs of instant memory recall.

"I'd appreciate it very much if you didn't kill her, Mr. Shine," I said. "Miss Hill is wanted as a suspect on a murder rap down in L.A. and maybe one up here. It will hurt my case a lot if I lose her."

"Murder rap, huh?" Shine said, interested. "Who was it, shamus—Witter?"

"It's beginning to look that way," I said.

Shine smiled blandly, for him. "Okay, she talks, maybe I don't kill her. You wanna try?"

I snapped my fingers. "How about it, Miss Hill? Mr. Shine just made you a very generous offer. Where's the package Felix gave you?"

Her eyes blazed angrily at me. "I don't know what you're talking about. Felix wasn't a dope smuggler any more than I am. You're both wasting your time if you think—"

Shine muttered something nasty and moved my chest farther away with his fingertips. He slapped her again, this time with his right hand on her near cheek. She made a small sound after bouncing off the wall, but it wasn't the one Shine wanted and he backhanded her to her original position.

I looked glumly around Shine's office. It looked like any typical warehouse office, cluttered with ledgers and sales slips on metal spikes, filing cabinets and a steel safe. In a box on his desk was Shine's only visible concession to his energy-consuming habit: light bulbs in varying sizes.

Shine stood between me and the gun on his desk as if wanting me to go for it so he could break me in half. But what Parson had already done to my body made me a trifle reluctant to give my all for the obstinate Miss Hill two times running in the same night.

I heard the sounds coming from Shine's big hands and wished to hell the vitamin broad had enough sense to know when to quit and tell him what he wanted to know. She took another tooth-rattling head shot and tottered toward me, her face white where it wasn't mottled with red streaks. Her lower lip was mashed and bleeding but set defiantly enough for Shine to slap her head off without her giving up and talking.

Shine sighed heavily and picked the big automatic off his desk. He brushed me aside easily with a sweep of his thick arm. "Stay outta the way, shamus. I think I'm through foolin around with this dumb broad."

I sat on his desk watching him cock his arm with the .45, ready to pistol-whip her now. I dropped one of the light bulbs on the stone floor and it exploded with a loud report. Shine turned, surprised, and I smashed another bulb squarely between his eyes. I stopped his scream with a kick where no man ever wants to be kicked, vital spot in the body *(kyusho),* and as he bent over, added *hizagashara-ate*—attacking vital spots with the kneecap.

Shine's face was a bloody mask as he toppled headfirst toward his desk, and I applied hand technique with fist edge at the base of his neck, crunching the greater occipital nerve, third occipital nerve and sternomastoid with elbow *(hiji).*

Shine slid slowly to the cement floor, looking as good as dead. I took the gun out of his relaxed fingers and turned to Miss Debbie Hill. "Please scream, Miss Hill, and maybe we can both get out of here alive."

Her eyes regarded me with the same unyielding displeasure. "What on earth for? You've managed to knock the man out and you have his gun."

I sighed, remembering that Dr. Yamada Yasushi, Seventh Dan of the Kodokan, had once observed that in attacking there are thirty-eight methods, which, applied to right or left, makes a total of seventy-six. Further, he noted that there were eighty *atemi* spots susceptible to attack. But he died without divulging which would be best for a stubborn woman.

I opted now for imperturbability of mind in emergency (*fudoshin*) and hit the switch on the wall, throwing the office into darkness. Miss Hill didn't scream at that, either, and I opened the door and called softly into the darkness.

"Lew, Charley—you better come in here, fast."

They came rushing in like lemmings, accepting me somehow now as part of the family. I tapped Lew on the side of the skull first and as he was falling, leveled a little harder on Charley, remembering his two previous scores on my sore noggin. Charley grunted, looked at me surprised and brought his gun up.

I hit him harder this time than I wanted to and he felt it enough to go down quietly. "Okay," I told Miss Hill.

She didn't answer and I tried again. She didn't do any better this time and I reached for the light switch, found it and flipped it up. There was nobody in Shine's office but me and him and Lew and Charley. Then I heard the clatter of running feet on the warehouse concrete floor and I recognized them immediately as those of the vitamin broad in flight.

I still had Mr. Shine's heavy automatic in my hand with a full load and could have dropped her, but I remembered she was still the prettiest suspect I had, and I didn't do anything but swear.

Twenty-four

Camino managed to disguise his normal feelings of happiness and camaraderie at the sound of my voice.

"Where you calling from?" he asked.

"I'm back. L.A. My hometown and yours. Just thought I should check with you before wrapping this up."

"Not a bad idea," he said. "What do you have so far? Let's try to keep it in the area of probability."

I filled him in and Camino heard me out without hanging up. "Is that it?" he said finally. "All you've got?"

"Well, I've been moving a lot. I thought maybe you might have come across something I've been too busy to notice."

"A few things," he said. "I'm hoping you can prove you didn't drop that gate on Frannie Corbett because she thought your hair was getting a bit thin on top."

"She never mentioned it. She was too dead."

"Then there are a lot of bodies up San Francisco way. There's that professor up in Berkeley . . ."

"Freddie Guest. I've an idea now who killed him, Nick."

"So far you're your own best suspect there. It's kind of a shame, too, because he never was that big a threat between you and Debbie Hill. Witter had better reasons but he died first. Knowing your devious mind, you could have planned it that way."

"You're kidding. Miss Hill knows more about all that than I can ever hope to. I'm sure she can clear this up if you had a few words with her."

"I already did, first thing this morning when she called me. You're an old friend, so I wouldn't want to begin to tell you the things she rapped you with."

"Let's hear it. Maybe it will help my end."

"Well, first, there's absolutely no question about your killing Parson. Beat him up savagely, Miss Hill said, threw him out a third-story window, didn't notify the authorities—like that, for openers."

"The girl's an ingrate, Nick. How else do you rescue a helpless girl in Chinatown?"

"Then there's aiding and abetting her abduction with Shine's boys, evading the authorities, delivering her as a prisoner to Shine, encouraging Shine to beat her up on a trumped-up charge that she stole his dope, killing Shine out of resentment after she had nearly convinced him she was an innocent dupe, trying to hand her over to Shine's hit men to prevent her escape—you want to hear more?"

"No," I said. "Maybe you see things from a different angle after you take too many vitamins."

"Well, there's just a bit more, from my own end. The girl's apartment . . . have any idea who ripped it apart?"

"That was one of the things I was hoping you'd tell me."

"Maybe it was Shine's boys, and maybe not. Care to tell me who you're moving in on from here?"

"I'd like to kill Doc Shipman. He more or less certified his niece was all right."

"I met the girl. So far she's an innocent bystander to me unless and until you can prove otherwise."

"Just another call or two," I said. "I think I'm hot onto her bag now. Then we'll be getting back to Miss Hill."

"I don't want to sound like a total ingrate," Camino said. "Thanks for Parson."

"That's what Charley said."

"Who's Charley?"

"Shine's top soldier. I hope I didn't kill him, too."

"No, but there's enough you have to account for already without him. Seriously, pal, you've got to come up with a big one and you've about run out of time."

"My very thoughts."

Mrs. Marilyn Channing was as blond and beautiful as I remembered her. She answered her door, looking my battered features over carefully before showing a sign of recognition.

"I think you looked better last time after messing up your breakfast," she said.

"Eggs are no contest. They don't hit back. May I come in, Mrs. Channing?"

She swung the door open wider. "If you think you're up to it."

I followed her incredibly slim waist and tantalizing butt across the padding on the floor, keeping a tight grip on my arteries.

The apartment was high, wide and handsome, furnished with the kind of taste a good deal of money can ensure. If Felix Witter had nicked her for the quarter mill, the lady apparently had oodles left and didn't appear to be hurting. I had to figure Frank Channing as a very good and generous loser.

She sat down gracefully on a long white sofa and waved me to a large chair opposite where I could have a better view of her sensational legs.

"Is this visit business?" she said, looking the least bit miffed when I nodded.

"When you came to see me, Mrs. Channing, you were interested in my finding out who killed Felix Witter. I'm wondering now if you're still of the same mind."

"Certainly." Her eyes left mine and strayed to her purse on a nearby table. "Do you have him?"

"Not yet but I'm reasonably close enough to close it out. There are a few details I'd like to get straight before going ahead, and you can help."

"We didn't discuss price," she said quickly, "but I can assure you—" She stopped as I waved my hands.

"That part of it can wait," I assured her. "As I understand it, you were referred to me by Miss Debbie Hill."

"Yes. I told you—"

My head was as good at going up and down as it was sideways. "The questions come into play because as I understand it, both Miss Hill and you seem to have been involved with Witter at the same time. Is that any kind of news to you?"

Mrs. Channing bit her luscious lower lip with sharp white teeth. "Not particularly, Mr. Roper. Felix Witter was inclined more or less favorably to any number of women. I'm reasonably certain Miss Hill was as aware of that aspect of him as I."

"True," I said, "or reasonably thereabouts. What I'm trying to establish now is the matter of priority, so to speak. Who was first in Mr. Witter's affections—you or Miss Hill? And again, conversely, who was seeing him last, toward the end?"

She had the long, gracefully turned leg balanced nicely on her other knee and swung it several times and it appeared to be working fine. "That's a very interesting question," she said. "There's no doubt at all in my mind that I knew Felix before Debbie Hill. I knew him at least for five years, starting before he broke up with his wife Kay. I was still married to Frank, and of course I wanted to be a lot surer before I dropped him for Felix."

"And in time you were?"

She smiled. "Not exactly. I found out that all I was sure of was that I wanted Felix any damn way I could get him, and I could get to see a lot more of him if I wasn't tied down to Frank. All clear?"

"Yes. Was any of that large sum you doled out to Witter given him about this time?"

"It was given to the bastard all the time. At the beginning, yes, particularly. But Felix always needed more, for one reason or another, and I was the prize patsy who had it."

"It's still a lot of money," I said. "Did he ever give you an accounting for what he did with it?"

"No, and I didn't expect any. I had the idea he was blowing most of it trying to start his own business, at first. But then he gave up the idea of going into business for himself and it didn't help much—he still needed an occasional sum."

I had a puzzle going. "It would seem to me that with that kind of drain going, you might have done better staying on with your husband. I'm speaking strictly from a money standpoint, and I'm kind of surprised Felix let you give up a good thing in the financial world like Frank Channing."

She laughed. "Your reasoning is absolutely perfect except for one little flaw."

"Better give it to me now before I get out too far ahead."

"*I* had the money, not the aforementioned Mr. Frank Channing."

I didn't have much face left with to work expressions of rue and so on. "*You* had the money?"

"My family is from Pasadena, Mr. Roper. My father and his family were rather large in some of the more basic commodities —like silver mines. And some oil, of course."

"Those would be good ones. But you're not saying that Mr. Channing married you for your money, are you?"

"Well, it's true, all right, but he happened to be a little better at business than Felix, that's all. What money Frank got from me went a very long way with him. He became a very successful investment broker, and short of a minor crisis or two every so often, he did all right on his own."

I took the loss and tried going around. "Getting back to Felix Witter and his romantic interests—you weren't put out when he began seeing Debbie Hill?"

Marilyn Channing made a wry face. "If it wasn't her, it would be somebody else. When you took on somebody like him, you had to be very realistic about the situation. I mean, the man was adored, idolized, wherever he went, all over the world. Whatever Debbie got out of him, she was lucky—or otherwise, as the case may have been."

"No hard feelings, no jealousies . . . little things of that nature? Just a very friendly all-girl person contest?"

"Something like that." She looked me over and didn't begin to tremble. "You seem skeptical."

"Yes, ma'am. That kind of friendly goings-on between various ladies wanting the same gent is very rare, and maybe is still something for the future. It seems to me with Felix needing the kind of money he was drawing, you might have felt well within your rights if he had drained a few of the other love slaves on the planet. Why just you?"

"I told you before. I wanted Felix any damn way I could get him."

"I don't get it," I said. "Granting that he was big, blond and beautiful—still, there were lots of other body beautifuls around. What was the world doing before Felix Witter came along? There's Eddie Blue available, Steve Shaw, a lot of others, even the has-beens like Johnny Albany. When Debbie latched on to your Felix, did you make use of your alternatives? Or did you just wait and suffer until Felix had time for you again?"

Her green eyes blazed. "Did you come up here to make moral judgments or are you trying to solve a murder?"

"Maybe they overlap, Mrs. Channing. I understand Felix had an abrasive personality. Rubbed people the wrong way and walked all over them. A man like that will take on a horde of people who hate his guts and would be happy to do him in."

"I suppose," she said. "A lot of them would be jealous of him, too."

"Right on," I said. "And despite all the many other reasons for knocking him off, I prefer to go with the old stand-bys—of thwarted love and affection. They're still good enough reasons for most of the murders. On that basis, with you and Debbie Hill vying for Witter's love and attentions, it would be a toss-up between you two to decide which of you killed him."

She looked at me unsmiling, very cool, and still very attractive in her soft feline way. "You may have a point there. Quite frankly, you're the kind of man I could easily love, too, and even more easily want to kill."

I shrugged. "I know you're there, too. But since I'm still alive and breathing, whereas Felix is not, let's concentrate on him. Your story, as I get it, is that you would have been content to let him bleed you forever, just so long as you could have him whenever he was available. Correct?"

"Something like that, although forever does seem quite a long time. I know there are plenty of other beautiful men around, or even hard types like you, but I was willing to wait on that. I'm sure that eventually I would have come to the end with Felix, but it was still in the future, and there would be plenty of time to look around then."

"You're telling me you didn't kill him?"

"Perhaps given a bit more time and frustration, I might have. But this time, you'll have to go on the premise that somebody else had other or better reasons for wanting him dead now."

I stood up and she did the same, more gracefully. We looked at each other but held our ground. I knew Marilyn Channing's own little timetable would let her know when to make the first step in my direction. It might be tomorrow, the next day, or whenever she decided to start a new conflagration.

"Forgetting crimes of passion for the moment," I said, "there's still plenty of book left for knocking Witter off. Do you think there was a chance he was engaged in trying to make an easy buck in dope smuggling?"

Her red lips curled derisively. "Felix? Mr. America, Mr. Universe, and God knows what all else? Are you serious?"

"I think I'm very serious."

"With that image that he worked so hard on? Hard work and exercise, no smoking, no drinking—the wholesome clean type? He would have had to be crazy, for one thing, and for another, I don't think he was subtle or complicated enough to have been able to manage such a careful deceptive life."

"It's happened," I said. "There's big money in dope and Felix liked money. Maybe he had the notion that someday you might stop feeding him, and he'd be on his own. The lecture circuit and the testimonials don't pay all that much. Maybe he thought a profitable sideline wouldn't be that bad an idea."

She tucked back a stray hair and smiled. "I thought we had both agreed there are other women around who are wealthy and insane enough to indulge a habit like Felix. As you suggested, he could have taken his business and beautiful body elsewhere. Why attempt something so contrary to his own ideals? Felix felt very strongly about the kids hooked on drugs. He was trying to live his life as an inspiration to them."

"I know," I said. "That's how he happened to be so good at two-timing every woman who thought she loved him."

Her cheeks colored now. "What more can I say? I've already debased myself in your eyes, haven't I?"

"Not too much," I said. "I'm not making judgments on you. Tell me something about his business. The one where he tried to compete but couldn't cut it."

"He rented a small building that had a lab. I advanced him the money he needed for the necessary materials. That was pharmaceutical equipment, as I recall."

"Would you remember where it was located, Mrs. Channing?"

She could and did, and I took it down. She took a step closer now and her green eyes were dancing and dangerous. "Is there anything else?"

I shook my head. "I don't think so. I'll be getting back to you. Letting you know when I have something, and so forth."

"Do that," she said. "I'm looking forward to it."

Then she stepped into my arms and it wasn't that difficult at all to kiss her.

Twenty-five

The switchboard person at the Healthfare Organics site for vitamin goodies remembered me and asked if Mr. Albany was expecting me. I said no, but would appreciate his time. She relayed most of this and passed me through her swinging gate.

He hadn't aged much in the past few days and sat straight at his desk moving his hands in a pool of correspondence, order forms and checks. His dark, intent eyes checked mine out before he got to his feet and put the crusher on my hand.

"Back again, sport? What's on your mind this time?"

"I'm still working on the Witter case. But a lot's happened since I saw you, and I thought you'd be interested in the developments."

"Well, sure, pal. I got a few minutes to spare. Shoot."

He waved me to a chair near his desk and settled back onto his behind the desk. "You may not like what I have to tell you," I said. "Not everybody likes to hear how they've been suckered."

Johnny Albany bared his white teeth in a flashing grin. "That'll be the day, when I learn I been the patsy. But let's hear. Maybe I got a lot to learn yet."

"It can happen to anybody. You get to know somebody and after a while it becomes natural to trust them. You do your own thing and keep your nose clean, and you figure the other party is playing the game the same way."

His eyes hardened. "Hold it, hold it. You trying to say Felix Witter suckered me?"

"I was taking the long way around. But he had a little help on the outside. And the other party was another you'd bet your bottom dollar was straight as a string."

He blinked furiously, thinking. "You got me there, for sure. What outside party you got in mind?"

"I'll have to tie it in first. Did you ever hear of a man called Shine? Ed Shine from up San Francisco way."

"No. What's he do?"

"Big underworld man. Worked all the rackets for years and lately found out how to make it big in narcotics."

Albany shook his dark curly head. "Never heard of him. And what's narcotics got to do with anything?"

"Not too much—except it's the main reason Felix Witter was murdered."

His look was disbelieving. "Come on. What're you giving me?"

I nodded confidently. "Felix Witter was working his own dope deals on the side, and thought he was big enough to take a shot at the real money. Shine had a big shipment of cocaine coming in. Felix heisted it—twenty-five million bucks' worth—with the aid of the other party, of course."

Albany tapped his desktop impatiently. "What other party?"

"You know her—Debbie Hill."

He stared. "Debbie? You're outta your mind."

"No. I've a pretty good case on her so far. Miss Hill was working closely with Witter on this coke deal. In our first interview after his death, she claimed she hadn't seen him in two months. Now she admits to having seen him as recently as two weeks ago—shortly before his death."

Johnny Albany was shaking his head, looking angry. "It's crap what you got, Roper—a lot of bull. Debbie would no more get into any kind of heist deal than the man inna moon. Witter? Well, maybe. Inna way I almost think it's possible, and I almost can go along with you on him trying to pull something to make a fast buck. But Debbie? Forget it, pal. Not unless you got some kind of proof."

"There's some of that, too. There was a state narcotics officer working between here and San Francisco working closely with my office, trying to get a line on a big-time smuggling ring. He had Debbie and Felix figured for it, and in fact had finally grabbed her yesterday, before Shine and his men could take her."

Albany shrugged. "Okay. So you wait and see. It'll blow up in this nark's face. Take my word for it, he won't have a thing on Deb. I know her too long. She's gotta be clean."

"It can't blow over. She got away from the state nark man."

His eyebrows lifted. "Jeez, how did that happen?"

"She called me from the apartment where he was holding her. I didn't know what it was all about then. When I got there, I found out the nark man has been playing it both ways, and wanted me out of the way too."

Albany's eyes narrowed. "You look a little beat up, my friend. So I guess you got away. What happened to Deb and the nark?"

I shrugged. "I had to kill him."

Albany whistled. "Hey, no kiddin!"

"I didn't have a choice. It was him or me."

"Okay, so if he was a fink, he deserved it. What happened to Deb?"

"Shine's men showed up and brought us back to his hangout. Shine didn't waste any time. He's been looking for her. He accused her of teaming up with Felix to make the heist. In fact, he claimed one of his men saw her the night it happened. The night Witter slugged his two delivery men and got away with the bundle."

Albany looked dazed. "How much you say it was worth?"

"According to Shine, twenty-five million bucks' worth of pure!"

He made rapid mental calculations. "But it would sell for more, right?"

"On the street, after it's been cut, yes—perhaps for ten times that amount."

155

"I can't believe it! Okay, I guess Shine made her cough it up, right?"

I shook my own head. "I was wrong about that, too. I thought he'd make her talk for sure. But she kept denying it, trying to have him think he was making a big mistake."

I was reaching Johnny Albany, getting him excited. "Deb was trying to hold out on this guy Shine? A big mobster?"

"One of the biggest in that area."

"Jesus, so what happened? You leave her up there with the guy?"

"No. I got her out of it."

"How the hell did you do that? Did she promise—"

"No. Shine was slapping her around. I had to break it up."

He stared, taking in every bump and contusion on my map. "Yeah—how?"

"I had to kill Shine."

Albany whistled a long flat note. "Jesus! I better not get you mad, looks like, huh?"

"No reason why you'd have to," I said, smiling. "But I came here directly to warn you. Debbie got away from me up there and she's back in town now. I had the notion she might be approaching you next, to help her get rid of the stuff."

"Huh? Why me?"

"I think Shine scared her. She knows now she's not good enough to handle it alone. She didn't think that far ahead apparently when she poisoned Witter's body oil and knocked him off so she could have all the stuff he had entrusted to her."

His eyes widened to their limits. "Debbie killed Felix? Hey, you feeling all right, pal? She was nuts about the guy."

"Maybe she was at one time. Maybe she even ditched him a few months ago, as she claimed. But when Felix called her two weeks ago to do him one last favor, he sealed his own death."

"How do you figure that?" Albany said, still showing a lot of skepticism.

"It all seems to tie in with that meeting. My guess is that Felix panicked some after knocking off Shine's men and taking the

156

stuff. And he left it with Deb to hold for him until he was ready to take it, when things cooled off some."

"You said she was supposed to be in on the heist with him. Somebody saw her."

I shrugged. "That could have been a guess. It was night—foggy in that area off the water. It could have been her or some other dame. But taking her part of the story for truth, I think she didn't know what Felix was sticking her with then, but later she heard about it, got nervous, wanted to unload.

"Felix might have started his biggest con job then on her, explaining how they could cut the stuff and get out of it with an awful lot of money. It wouldn't take much thinking for Debbie then to decide she didn't need him for that part of the operation. And she went ahead and killed him."

Albany's brow wrinkled trying to follow the plot outline. "Well, yeah, I happen to know Felix had a lot of other birds in his stable. Maybe Deb wasn't too happy about that, neither. Maybe she put the pressure on him then to unload the other talent, and stick with her alone—or else."

I liked that thought from Albany, wondering if the same idea hadn't occurred to Marilyn Channing. The difference was that Debbie had to be operating from a stronger position, with the very expensive product in her possession, while all Mrs. Channing had to bargain with was her own loot.

I nodded to Albany. "From what I've heard of Witter, he would have laughed at her, maybe even slapped her around to get her to learn her place."

"Yeah," Albany said softly. "I seen the bastard operate with dames. Funny thing is, he could slap them silly and they still come back asking for more."

"But not Miss Hill, apparently. And now, she's had a period in which to think it all over. And my hunch is she's coming to you very soon, and you'd better be ready."

Albany exploded. "Jesus, I asked you before—why me? She knows I wouldn't deal in no dope. I been in the health-food racket nearly ten years now. You think I want to take a chance on a bust now, just when everything is looking good?"

157

"We're talking about twenty-five million dollars cut maybe ten times, Johnny. For that kind of money, a lot of men might consider letting go of a business they liked."

He whistled again. "Holy mackerel—yeah, I see what you mean. Only again, why me? We ain't never been sweet on each other, y'know."

"Miss Hill has a warm feeling in her heart for big strong men. You're not that much out of shape as you might think. And a Mr. America, even a former one, could still look mighty attractive to her."

He didn't puff out his chest or preen. "Well, yeah, but there's a lotta other guys around don't look too bad neither. There's Eddie Blue for one, Steve Shaw—"

I held up one finger and Albany cocked his head to focus on it. "There's a lot of healthy, good-looking muscle around, sure. But what you have is what Debbie needs. And you're the only one who's got it."

"Got what?"

I waved my arms expansively, embracing his total plant. "You've got the Johnny Albany sure-fire method for distribution. Healthfare Organics. Who else is there around to match you?"

He shook his head puzzledly again. "What're you on to now? Me—my company distribute dope for Debbie Hill?"

I stepped off a few paces and reached out to the glass shelf with the product. Johnny Albany's line still had the top-shelf-priority position, and Witter's High-Protein bottles were below. I picked up one of Witter's.

I shook the bottle in front of Albany's face, "The stuff I'm talking about looks so much like this powder, you couldn't tell the difference unless you smelled it or had a chemical breakdown.

"Shine's missing heist comes down to about a hundred pounds now. You've got pint, quart and gallon containers of your stuff in your warehouse, to be moved out to different companies and stores. Who would know if you managed to slip a chosen number carefully marked and labeled to select points for pickup?"

He was off his seat as if jet-propelled, and a few lithe steps had him at my side. He took the small bottle of Witter's protein powder from my hand. He spun his strong fingers, and the bottle cap didn't argue and came off. Albany looked down at the white powder, sniffed it, then spilled a small amount off into his hand.

"Jeez, y'mean it looks like this?"

"A lot like that. It's fine and powdery and flaky. But packed inside a colored bottle, nobody would ever spot it. The same goes for heroin. It looks very much like what you've got in your palm."

He kept shaking his head. "That stuff, too? Jesus!" He kept staring at the mound of fine-powdered particles in his hand, sniffed it again, then carefully funneled it back into the original small bottle.

Replacing the product on the shelf, he reached down to a lower level and picked up a quart-container size. It was labeled High-Protein Powder and was in a large can. He pried the lid off and stared down at the contents. He took a deep breath, shook his head and replaced the lid, and then the can on its shelf.

Albany faced me squarely now, fists jammed on his hips. "Okay, let's say I got the way to make it move. Debbie thinks I'm gonna fall for her pitch and brings me the whole operation. What the hell I do then? Throw her out? Call the FBI?"

I shook my head. "No, you don't do any of those. You act interested until she shows you the key."

His handsome, swarthy features clouded again. "Key? What the hell key?"

"The key Felix Witter gave her after he stashed Shine's product in a safe place."

"I don't get it. What safe place? His pad, you mean?"

I shook my head. "That wouldn't be nearly safe enough. A lot of houses and apartments get broken into. But a locker at a bus station is generally a pretty safe place to leave a package overnight, or for a short period of time."

Albany thought about it out loud. "That's right. You put in your luggage or whatever, turn the knob, take out the key. To get it out, you put in the coins and turn the key . . ."

I nodded comfortingly. "So you don't do any business with Miss Hill at all, until she can show you the key. And when you get that far, I'd appreciate a call before you go along with her to pick it up."

His brow wrinkled. "Y'mean you don't trust me?"

"It's not that, Johnny. When I left Shine dead up there, I made the mistake of leaving two of his hit men alive. They know all about Miss Hill and the missing heist and what it's worth, and they'll still be looking. So you'll be a lot safer with me and the regular federal agents taking the load off your hands."

He wiped his glistening brow with the back of his hand. "Jeez, yeah, I never thoughtta that. Okay, sure. Leave your number. I'll get back to you soon as she lets me know she's got it."

Twenty-six

The call came later that evening and Johnny Albany sounded excited. "Jesus, you were right, Roper. Debbie called, just like you said. I couldn't believe it."

"How did she put it to you?"

"Well, that was far out, too. It's almost like I never knew her like I thought I did. I mean, she about came right out with it."

"You mean, about having Shine's product?"

"Oh no, not that. But kind of leading up to it, you know? First thing she said, she was thinking of leaving her Good Earth Things vitamin house. That she was just wasting time pushing the same old buttons, getting nowhere. And considering her experience and know-how in promotion, and with Felix out of it at my place, maybe we could work something out to our mutual benefit. Like that."

"And you bit?"

He laughed. "You kidding? Deb knows me too well for that. She knows I'm supposed to be sharp, so naturally I can't be no pushover. I mean, what the hell kind of deal is she offering me? Because she's talking like partnership, you dig? And when you're talking partners, you're talking about buying in. So I act cool, ask her what she's got to offer."

A glance at my watch told me it was ten o'clock, and I wondered if it was going to be the same witching hour once more, midnight.

Albany gave me a little time to digest his material, then had more to say. "Now get this, sport. She doesn't say she has money. She doesn't even ask me how much it costs to buy in to Healthfare Organics. What she says is, whatever it takes to make a deal, she's got. You hear that? Before I even run through any kind of numbers, she's already got it.

"Now, when she says this, I know you gotta be right. Because I know the kind of job Deb had these five, ten years, she couldn't be laying that much aside. If she makes two bills a week, she's getting a lot from that cheap bastard Shelby. Maybe two fifty, so he could have her around to look at. But even that don't make it, right?

"So I ask her right out. I ask who's behind her, who's backing her. Fair question, right? That way, she knows I'm still Johnny A, and not acting like no dummy because a well-stacked chippie wants to do me a favor by buying in."

"Okay, what did she say?"

"She says she's not at liberty to discuss that at the moment. But if I'm willing to meet her and discuss her proposition, she'll show me all the proof I need, that she's got what it'll take. Now, that's crazy, ain't it? Why be so damn mysterious? You're talking money—well, either you got it or you don't. A guy or a bank backs you or not. So what the hell is she talking about?"

"Tell me where she's going to meet you, and maybe I can come up with a better guess."

"All right. She says Felix's old lab. Jesus, I forgot the guy once rented one years ago. I never knew he still kept it up. Talk about not knowing somebody you thought you could trust, pal, you sure hit it right on the button."

"The lab in Manhattan Beach?"

"Yeah. How did you know about that?"

"I think Marilyn Channing told me."

"Oh yeah. Well, sure, she was feeding him whatever bread he needed, I guess she would know. Okay, so what d'ya figure?"

"It's simple, Johnny. Miss Hill most likely will show you some of the dope Witter already had on hand, cut and decked.

162

Stacked bundles that will bring in a lot of money once it goes out to the buyers."

"That much money?"

"It doesn't take much of that stuff to make a lot of money, Johnny. Four pounds of heroin sells on the street for quarter of a million bucks. Seven and a half pounds of cocaine is worth two million. If she's got some hashish that Witter might have been dealing in, we've found that stuff packed in little cashew-nut tins. Twenty-five of them were worth over twenty million bucks. Get the picture?"

"What if the stuff is cut already and I don't know the difference?"

I laughed. "It's already been cut several times, most likely. But you're supposed to be looking, not buying. If you want to act hip, twenty-four bags of seventy-three percent pure cocaine has a value on the street of ten million dollars."

Albany's whistle shrilled in my good ear. "You think Felix was dealing that big?"

"It's beginning to look like it. He had the money to invest, his own lab for cutting the stuff, and his own ways of getting it out on the street."

"Man," Albany said, "if he's got that kind of action going, why does he take a chance going against a tough mobster like this guy Shine up there?"

"What I keep hearing over and over again about Felix was that he would do anything for a buck. And Shine's stuff was pure, remember, worth so much money it was worth the try. It would be worth hijacking to plenty of other people besides Felix Witter. For all we know, Shine might have stolen it from somebody else."

"Okay, I get the picture. So here's the deal we set up. I'm meeting her down at the old lab. But I think maybe you ought to be there, just in case. I mean, what if the joint is raided? There sits Johnny A, with all that hot dope. If Debbie is such a double-crossing broad, she could be setting me up for something too. Right?"

163

"It's possible," I said, finding it hard to believe any of this. "What time is the meeting?"

"She said midnight."

"I'll be there."

There was still time before the big dope face-off at the old lab between my most improbable suspect and the man who might at last clear the air. There was time to recall one of the basic tenets in the detective business, to the effect that it never hurts to have evidence, and even a little is better than none. So far, what I had on Felix Witter was garbage, strictly speaking. A lot of hearsay and coincidental goings-on, coupled with the kind of deductive imagination done far better in fortune cookies.

I conned a friendly phone operator into revealing the exact location of his new pad in Manhattan Beach, and wheeled off in hopes that I might luck on to something incriminating.

Witter's house was a few blocks off the residential tree section on a high bluff overlooking the water. There were two other houses on the dark street, on the slope below, a light or two showing, and I risked the chance that they didn't know much more about Witter than I did.

The side patio was littered with sand, beach chairs, dumbbells and barbells holding different weights. My mini-burglar kit got me through the glass doors, and I hit the wall switches so I wouldn't miss a trick.

The interior ran more to a beach bum's idea of opulence than a well-heeled sybarite's. The furnishings were sparse, early Salvation Army or Goodwill, and the floor had more dumbbells lying around than King Solomon. The front room was large and spacious, as it had to be for a man of Witter's dimensions; the kitchen was small and littered with boxes.

There were two bedrooms upstairs. One was stacked with more boxes Witter had still not unpacked, reaching from wall to wall, gleanings from his past quarters. The other was his working bedroom, and again nothing. No overhead mirror, no animal-skin bedspread, no erotic colored sheets, and it was apparent that with all the muscles he had, Witter figured that was enough for his playmates to look at. The bed was king-size, as it nearly had to be for a man his bulk, but of course smaller men, too, have favored the larger edition as their battlefield with the sex persons of their choice.

The walk-in closets provided no evidence that Witter was going to be the well-dressed man of any year. A couple of cheap suits, scruffy shoes, some beach robes, a tattered bathrobe. Much more in evidence were the sneakers and shorts, the short-sleeved polo sport shirts, warm-up suits, sweat shirts and windbreakers, jockstraps and bathing trunks.

The bathroom was a hypochondriac's dream. All the lotions and liniments, oils and sprays and gargles that would keep a man well, glistening and supple. Skin creams, hair creams, deodorants, hair sprays, foot-ease powders and fumigants. Jars of aspirin, wheels of gauze and tape, disinfectants, antihistamines, antiseptics, germicides and gargles.

There was one dull razor blade in his razor, and one spare on the shelf. No fancy colognes or perfumes for milady, as some bachelors will do it, and the towels came out of the dime store. Whatever Felix Witter had done with the $200,000 Marilyn Channing had given him, not more than a farthing had gone into the house, and only the drugstore had profited.

A battered dresser held his socks and underwear, and he had enough there easily to go away on any three-day convention. I went back into the spare bedroom and broke open some of the boxes. There were more trophies and silver loving cups than I could count: belts, bracelets, plaques and awards.

Like any champ who has had to wade through the prelims, Witter had come along slowly, winning an occasional Best Leg or Best Lats or Best Abdominals from various minor towns and counties, before he won the intersectionals and became the Mr. Best at everything, after he had put it all together.

There were photographs of him, leaner in some, grossly overweight in others, as he fought his way up, muscling himself deeper and thicker, contouring his body to be exactly the way he wanted it to be at the end. Snapped glossies of Witter with officials, township bigshots, with arms spread around long-haired adoring young bunnies.

There wasn't any dope in any of the boxes, no more dope than a lot of how-to books on exercising and training, lifting weights, breathing and physical-fitness manuals. I breezed through the upstairs, checking out everything but the toothpaste tubes, finding nothing more incriminating than that Felix Witter was a sloppy, stingy, carefree man who apparently thought of nothing more exciting than his own body.

Marilyn Channing had said he liked expensive threads, but perhaps she had needed that as some kind of sop to her pride. She had said she never asked where the money went, didn't care, and now that he was dead she wanted his killer, and I had to know.

Maybe the lab ate up a lot of the ready money Mrs. Channing made available, or maybe he blew it at the track or up at Vegas. I'd be able to check that out another time, but I wanted something concrete before I met with Johnny Albany and Miss Hill.

He didn't have any first editions, old masters or expensive jewelry. A man who makes over fifty grand a year by just flexing his muscles in six different positions, who owns only two razor blades and a pair of socks, and still has to take oodles from a dame has to be doing something exceptional with the money. Something apart from and beyond his life style.

I tried the kitchen fridge, wondering if he'd possibly put it all in good caviar. There wasn't any more in the icebox than a hard piece of cheese, an apple, a carrot, a wilted piece of lettuce, a container of sour milk, and a jar of the Felix Witter High-Protein powder mix.

I took the lid off and dipped a finger in and tasted it. My taste buds told me it was bitter and I said "Eureka!" because heroin tastes bitter.

The gas station down the street had a phone booth. I called my friend Camino and persuaded him to make a phone call.

"She can always tell me to drop dead, you know," he complained.

"That's okay," I said. "At least, you'd be hearing it for the first time."

Twenty-seven

Witter's lab was a low concrete-block building nesting close to a health club for women. It was midnight and I was the only one out for exercise. There were two cars parked in the back lot. Their hoods were hot. I added mine to the lot.

The rear door was steel and locked. I rattled the knob and it opened with Johnny Albany looming behind in a long dark hallway. Behind his broad shoulders, I could see the lit lab section. He pulled me in with a hearty back slap, then closed the door behind me. I heard the double clicking sound.

Albany grinned. "I'm locking it, pal. If the skirt set me up tonight, nobody gets through this steel door in a hurry."

The lab off the hallway was a long glass box lit by overhead banks of fluorescent tubes. It wasn't as bright as the late Mr. Shine's warehouse, but then, neither was I. Johnny Albany ushered me through the glass door and closed it behind us. His hand flipped to the dark-haired girl sitting on a high stool lab perch, watching me enter without visible delight in her eyes.

"You remember Debbie Hill," he said.

I nodded. "Nice to see you up and around again, Miss Hill. How are things in the dope field?"

"I'm hoping they'll be better after I find out what this is all about tonight," she said rather sharply.

I looked at Albany, surprised. "I thought you said everything was set."

He shook his head, looking worried, biting his lip. His hands pleaded for understanding. "I thought so, too. Maybe she cooled. How about if you took care of your end of it—you know, get that big part out of the way first, huh?"

"The Shine shipment?"

He nodded, heaving his chest gratefully. "Yeah. That number. I can't tell if she's bluffing."

I shrugged it off. "It could be Miss Hill is shy because of the personal element. I'll do my end of it fast and get out of the way so you can discuss your own business."

"I can hardly wait," Miss Hill said. "You become more bizarre every time we meet. I warned you about how drinking can drain the vitamin B reserves from your body. Your brain cells become starved."

"First things first, Miss Hill, and my body will have to learn to adjust. At our last meeting, the question of what happened to Mr. Shine's shipment of pure cocaine went begging and unresolved. I have the odd notion that perhaps unwittingly you were a dupe for Felix Witter."

Her thin eyebrows lifted a shade. "You said dupe—not dope?"

"It could be both. Felix had something he had to hide, something that was potentially very injurious to his health to carry. So he parked it and asked you to hold the means whereby he might one day, when the heat was off, reclaim it. I'm referring specifically to a key to a locker, most likely one in the San Francisco bus station and air terminal building at Taylor and O'Farrell."

A thin vertical line formed between her arched brows. "A key?" she repeated.

I nodded. "The key opens the locker. The locker contains about a hundred pounds of pure cocaine belonging to the late Mr. Shine, valued by the aforesaid Mr. Shine to the tune of twenty-five million bucks.

"Felix Witter made the heist. He panicked when Shine's men began trailing him, and parked it at the terminal, hoping for better days. One of the men that he sandbagged identified you as

Witter's helper that night, but now it's immaterial. That witness died. But that key in your possession now links you with the goods. It's a punishable offense to deal with narcotics in any way. I'm an investigator working with state and federal narcotic agents and am empowered to arrest you by reason of the charge."

I withdrew my billfold and flashed the news in her face. She studied it, thought about it awhile, then shrugged. "Well, for goodness sakes, why on earth didn't you say so before?"

I restrained my answer and waited while she dipped into her purse. Her hand came out holding a key. She dropped it into my extended palm.

"Thank you, Miss Hill. I can't speak for Mr. Shine, but I can assure you the government appreciates your cooperation."

She slid off the stool. "And now I'm free to go?"

I nodded. "And may your children never take vitamins."

Johnny Albany's powerful frame blocked the door. "What the hell's going on, Roper? You letting her go? Didn't she kill Felix?"

I shook the old head. "No, Johnny. You did."

He stared. "Me? You gotta be kidding."

"You killed a lot of people, Johnny. Besides Felix Witter, you killed a friend of mine, an agent named Dill. You killed Professor Freddie Guest, a friend of Miss Hill's, up at Berkeley. And you got another score at Dante's hair salon when you killed the girl stylist who was the contact for Felix, Frannie Corbett. So far you've killed more people than I have. I suppose I'm jealous."

His dark face tightened. "Come on, pal. What the hell you trying to pull here? You know the dame here did it all. You had it all figured before when we talked. How come the switch?"

I showed him the little metal key in my hand. "I had to con you some because I needed this to get Shine's dope before you did. As it turns out, it looks like Felix was the big dope dealer we were looking for, and you were in it with him. Whatever reasons you had for killing him would have to be more than Miss Hill had.

"You had to kill the rest of them because alive they were all links in the chain leading to your working with Witter. But it's your funeral now, Johnny. And I guess it fits that you get buried right here. In the lab you pretended you didn't know a thing about it. A good cover for a pair of bright dope dealers."

I looked down the long white tables and glass counters at the beakers and mixers, and the jet-nozzle hoses of acetylene gas containing the burning melting flame. His gun was out when I got back to him.

It was a black automatic, the Garcia Beretta M 70, good for a six-shot load of .38-caliber instant death with its reputation for true firing. He couldn't have missed at this range unless he suddenly came down with palsy, and I couldn't depend on Johnny Albany, a former Mr. America and lifetime vitamin buff to get the shakes at this critical point in his career.

Guns pointed in my face generally make me nervous. At this stage even more so, because you can be shot full of holes before you leave your suspect dumfounded and contrite with the unerring logic of your summation. "Starting with Felix Witter, my guess is you found out he was into dope a while back. Cutting the stuff here, and getting it out to carefully selected setup points, using your facilities and distribution.

"When you found out, at first you thought it would ruin you and your rep. But Felix talked you out of your mad by cutting you in on the action. You had a tiger by the tail, but it was big money and you didn't want to let go of it.

"After you learned his methods, I suppose you wanted a bigger cut. Felix didn't go along, so you decided to kill him and go it alone. That was easy for you because he had modeled all his training habits on yours when you were top dog. You could have switched the poison bottle for his regular rubbing oil while he was in your office discussing some business you arranged just before he went on to the Mr. Universe contest."

"You knew Witter was using Frannie Corbett as his contact, letting her pass it along to her customers at Dante's during the day, or leaving the back door open the nights she worked alone. Our agent Dill got wise to what was going on, and when you got word from her about his nosing around, you knocked him off. Eventually you had to take her out, too, with that goddamn gate before she had a chance to talk to me and link you with Felix Witter.

"I'm sure you wasted the professor up in Berkeley, but I can't figure that one out, other than that Guest was another link associating you and Felix with the dope. Miss Hill had told me Felix was jealous of Freddie Guest, but he didn't kill him—you did. There was fifty grand worth of payoff money up in Guest's kitchen, and I had to figure that was for dope you and Felix sent his way for the Bay Area pushers.

"You had Miss Hill set for the next kill. You never could trust Felix and weren't sure how much she knew. Eventually if she guessed right about him, she would have to know you were part of the deal. But meanwhile you had killed Witter before you knew where he stashed Shine's coke. Maybe you even killed him because he was holding out on you.

"You lucked into it at the end because Miss Hill had me fooled. Some women do a lot of crazy things to hold on to a man they love, and I thought she was another in the deck.

"When you heard my story, I knew you wouldn't kill her before she produced the locker key. She called you, as you told me she would. But I still don't get the whole picture."

Albany blinked. "So what don't you get?"

"The fifty grand stashed in Guest's kitchen. I couldn't figure why you would leave all that money there."

The former Mr. America lifted his chest and grinned with a rueful headshake. "I left it there because I couldn't find it. I checked the damn kitchen. Where was it?"

"Upper cabinet, left side. In a coffee can."

He rubbed his jaw with his spare hand. "You don't figure it's still there, do you?"

"No way. I called the fuzz to report it. But you'll cash in on Shine's twenty-five million, so you won't need the lousy fifty thousand bucks. Why did you kill Guest?"

"Well," Albany said, "that was kind of interesting. What happened was, Felix really wanted to kill the guy first. But it wasn't over no dope. It was because of Deb. He really was jealous of the jerky prof. Can you imagine?

"It seemed dumb to me but I couldn't talk him out of it. So one day he went up there and started to push the guy around, you know how big Felix was, so it figures he scared the guy silly. Telling him if he ever saw Deb again what he would do, and so on. Then he got the bright idea. He worked out a deal with Guest. Told him if he took the stuff Felix sent up there, had it available when the pickup people came, he'd let him be. He even gave him a couple grand as a bonus. Feeding him a grand every so often when business was going good."

"The fifty grand was payola money for the dealer?"

Albany nodded. "Felix was dealing in everything: hash, pot, H and H-caps he made up here, coke, acid. Whatever he could buy, make or cut, he could unload."

"What about the head professor there—Dr. Holt—was he in on anything?"

Albany shook his head. "According to Felix, he was just dumb enough to be next. He had a crush on Deb, the old boy did, and Felix figured a little extra spending money might have done the trick, brought him in on the line."

I turned to Miss Hill. "Do you understand now why Parson and Shine were after you?"

"It all seems utterly crazy, but yes. It's clear enough to me now."

"In that case, I can give Johnny the key, and we're all square."

I tossed the key to his waiting hand and she screamed. "You idiot! Now he'll kill us!"

"Don't be silly," I said, turning away. "Johnny's got all he needs now to make him a very wealthy man. He doesn't have to kill anybody."

"No, sport, you're wrong," Albany said. "You both got too much on me. Sorry but I gotta kill you."

Twenty-eight

Camino nodded, showing little emotion, a typical example of a case-hardened cop who has seen and heard it all too often.

"Obviously he didn't," he said, yawning. "It's way past my bedtime but I'm willing to listen if you make it short."

Miss Hill looked at me and sighed. "I'm sleepy too. But I'm just curious about one thing. Why is it that every time I see you, some man is beating your brains in, really wiping the floor with you before you suddenly do something lucky and win?"

I shrugged with the one good shoulder I had left. "They don't play fair," I said. "They hit me before I'm ready. But if you really don't want to hear—"

"Come on," Camino said. "What the hell—so there you are with Albany's gun on you, only six shots away from permanent retirement, and—"

"Okay," I said, sniffing. "If you really want to hear it."

"I don't know why *I* have to hear it," Miss Hill said. "I saw it. The whole bloody mess. You really ought to take vitamins. Did you notice how easily he threw you around tonight?"

"Frankly, no," I said. "I was too busy to notice."

Camino's eyes began to close.

"All right," I said. "You'll remember I had turned away before he said the fatal words. I thought he would switch hands to catch the key I tossed. What I didn't know then was that Johnny Albany was a natural southpaw."

"Tough," Camino said. "A real tough break."

"I gave him back kick *(ushiro-geri)* and surprised him. It caught him high on the chest and knocked him back against the wall. His eyes were spinning and I thought he was going out. I had to get Miss Hill out of there fast, and I grabbed her arm and got her to the door. As far as I can remember, she was out the door before something hit me from behind. It wasn't her so it had to be him."

I bent forward and showed Camino the exact part of my skull where Johnny had made his first big hit. Camino nodded, clucking his tongue sympathetically, and I continued with the next few trips I had made to the floor, with Albany swinging from left field with astonishing speed for an old retired Mr. America and the kind of power all those years of body building had ensured for him, catching me more than he missed, sending me around the lab as if I was playing musical chairs all by myself.

"That karate is great stuff," Camino murmured, lighting a cigarette. "Too bad you never remember you majored in it."

"The last fall I took did it," I said. "He knocked me over the table. I came off holding the jet torch they use. He came after me and I turned the flame on and it bit him and he threw up his hands to protect his face."

Camino held up his hand. "Let me finish. I know your moves. You were on him like a tiger—"

"Well, yeah, I suppose . . ."

"You gave him foot-and-leg technique and knee kick to groin *(hiza-geri),* and when he bent forward, you did knife-hand strike to the face and followed with knife-hand strike to the collarbone and when that snapped, inverted-fist strike to the spleen *(uraken hizo-uchi),* and as he was going down, elbow strike—"

"No, Nick. Then I brought up my knee to his face *(hiza-uchi)* and—"

"Right," Camino said. "And then you remembered how he killed Dill, and gave him front kick and high kick and forefist strike to the chin *(seiken ago-uchi)* and somewhere in around there, Johnny Albany went down and died on you."

175

I nodded. "I guess he hemorrhaged internally and bled to death."

Camino nodded. "I suppose. But I got it right?"

"Well, all but the part about the key. When I came in and showed Miss Hill my open billfold, I had a note stuck in there for her to give me her mailbox key. That's what I tossed to Johnny Albany, you see?"

"What the hell difference did that make?" Camino barked. "He still had the gun on you and was about to kill you both."

"But if he did," I said, "he never would have got the twenty-five million bucks' worth of Shine's dope."

Twenty-nine

She looked about as beautiful as any woman you would want to see there.

"I hope you're not the jealous, possessive type," she said.

"Who, me? Never," I said.

"Because I know a lot of people, as I think I've already told you. And I have to travel a lot in my line of work."

"I know," I said. "But right now you're here and—"

"Well, I just wanted you to know. I wouldn't want there to be any misunderstanding."

"Hold it just one second," I said. I reached for the bottle on the nighttable by the bed and splashed some of the stuff into the glass and swirled it around. "I hear this stuff deadens the pain."

She lay there quietly watching me tilt the glass, swallow and then grimace. I grabbed for the bottle to check the label. "What the hell are they putting into this stuff now? This tastes worse than house Scotch."

"I didn't think you'd mind," she said. "I added a few vitamin B supplements while you were in the shower . . ."

About the Author

KIN PLATT was the newspaper cartoonist of the comic strip *Mr. and Mrs.* for the New York Herald Tribune Syndicate. His theatrical caricatures have also been featured in many newspapers and magazines. He is currently living in Los Angeles. He has written several popular juveniles, among them *Sinbad and Me*, which won the Edgar Award from the Mystery Writers of America for the best juvenile mystery of the year, and *The Boy Who Could Make Himself Disappear*, which was distributed as a major motion picture under the title *Baxter*. He has written five previous adult mysteries: four of them, *The Pushbutton Butterfly*, *The Kissing Gourami*, *The Princess Stakes Murder* and *The Giant Kill*, feature private eye Max Roper; in the fourth, *Dead as They Come*, there is Molly Mellinger, New York mystery editor and amateur detective.